THE MYTHICS

PAPERCUTZ

2. TEENAGE GODS

ALICE PICARD • JÉRÔME ALQUIÉ • FRÉDÉRIC CHARVE
PATRICK SOBRAL • PATRICIA LYFOUNG
PHILIPPE OGAKI • FABIEN DALMASSO

PAPERCUT*Z*
New York

Originally published in French under the following titles:
Les Mythics, volume 2, de P. Sobral, P. Lyfoung, P. Ogaki and A. Picard
Les Mythics, volume 5, de P. Sobral, P. Lyfoung, P. Ogaki, F. Dalmasso and J. Alquié
Les Mythics, volume 6, de P. Sobral, P. Lyfoung, P. Ogaki and F. Charve
© Editions Delcourt, 2018/2019
Created by PATRICK SOBRAL, PATRICIA LYFOUNG, and PHILIPPE OGAKI

Part I- Parvati
Script — PHILIPPE OGAKI
Art — ALICE PICARD
Color—MAGALI PAILLAT

Part 2- Miguel
Script —PATRICK SOBRAL with help from FABIEN DALMASSO
Art and Color — JÉRÔME ALQUIÉ

Part 3- Neo
Script —PHILIPPE OGAKI
Art —FRÉDÉRIC CHARVE
Color — MAGALI PAILLAT

Original editor — THIERRY JOOR

Special thanks to SÉVERINE AUPERT, LUCIE MASSENA, LINA DI FLAMMINIO, and JAYJAY JACKSON

Papercutz books may be purchased for business or promotional use. For information on bulk purchases please contact Macmillan Corporate and Premium Sales Department at (800) 221-7945 x5442

Translation — ELIZABETH S.TIERI
Lettering — WILSON RAMOS JR.
Production — BIG BIRD ZATRYB
Managing Editor — JEFF WHITMAN
Editorial Intern — ERIC STORMS
JIM SALICRUP
Editor-in-Chief

PB ISBN: 978-1-5458-0485-8
HC ISBN: 978-1-5458-0484-1

Printed in China
December 2020

Distributed by Macmillan
First Papercutz Printing

PART 4: PARVATI

Story by
PHILIPPE OGAKI

Art by
ALICE PICARD

Color by
MAGALI PAILLAT

A new album in the epic adventure that is THE MYTHICS. Thanks to you, dear readers, all the MYTHICS fans who have become loyal followers of this saga—thanks for having confidence in us. Thank you also to Fabien Dalmasso who was in charge of the difficult part of editing this script and an enormous thank you to Jérôme Alquié who agreed to give a body to my story; collaborating with him was a treat. And obviously, let's not forget Patricia Lyfoung, Philippe Ogaki and Delcourt, all at the core of this superb epic and all in this together for crazy adventures. What a path we've taken... And what a path still to come. But the best is yet to come!
—*Patrick Sobral*

A great THANK YOU to Patrick, Fabien, Philippe, and Jérôme for this beautiful volume of THE MYTHICS! Merci to the team at Delcourt who supported us since the beginning and thanks to whom we live this beautiful mythic adventure! Thanks to Fred for accepting to join us in the adventures of the Mythics! Thanks to Magali for the superb colors!
And thanks to you, our readers, for having this book in your hands... And for making this adventure mythic! Without you, we couldn't make a living from this beautiful profession!
—*Patricia Lyfoung*

I would like to thank the entire team of wonderful authors and friends who gave so much energy to bring life to the Mythics. I thank you, the reader as well, for your enthusiasm to accompany our young heroes in their adventures! I would like to thank all the people who went out of their way so that the Mythics could start their great adventures! In particular, Fred, who knew how to give life to Neo.
—*Philippe Ogaki*

Thanks to THE MYTHICS team, in particular Patricia, Philippe, and Thierry for having confidence in me and for their availability and help. Thanks to Magali for the work just in time.
—*Frederic Charve*

Thanks to all the readers who followed us during this season 1, looking forward to the next!
—*Magali Paillat*

Thanks to the entire Mythics team for their attention and their unfailing support. This was a marvelous adventure.
—*Fabien Dalmasso*

Thanks to the entire Mythics team, to the heart of Delcourt, and among the authors Patricia Lyfoung and Philippe Ogaki. And especially to Thierry Joor my director of the collection and of course Patrick Sobral, the genius author with whom collaboration was a true pleasure of apprenticeship and exchange. Your feedback and your advice were always precious and respectful, you are the best, gentlemen, don't change anything! Also a special thank you among the authors to Fabien Dalmasso who perfectly prepared my storyboard work and the final boards with very precise descriptions of each of the scenes.

Thanks to my family who accompanied me on each adventure, Cricri my better half that I love, Rémi, Maéline and Antonin, my three loves as well as my parents and my closest friends who always support me. Thanks to all my friends, you know who you are, Arnaud, Jean-Sé, Yvan, Jess, Lydie and everyone I'm forgetting...
And thanks to you, for reading this book, because it's obvious that we're only doing this work to bring pleasure and amusement to the public, and that we only exist thanks to you!
I hope that this book fascinates you as much as it did me while making it with the entire THE MYTHICS team.

PREVIOUSLY IN THE MYTHICS

An ancient evil returned to earth after being banished to Mars for millennia. The old gods who thought they had defeated Evil must find new young protectors on earth. Six children from all over the world were chosen…

First, *Yuko*, a Japanese schoolgirl in a rock band discovered she had electrifying lightning powers. She met her ancestor, Raijin, the god of lighting himself, who led Yuko to the legendary weapon. Yuko learned to hone her newfound powers of electricity to defeat Fujin, the evil god of wind, before he could destroy all of Japan with nuclear warfare.

Meanwhile, in Egypt, young *Amir*, a recently orphaned boy taking over his father's successful company and landholdings, encountered Horus, the Sun and Moon god. Horus and Amir struggled to vanquish Evil in the form of Seth (aided by Amir's wicked half-brother) after they reanimated all the dead mummies in an attempt to take over the world in Evil's image.

Then, a young Opera hopeful, *Abigail*, faced a blizzard freezing all of Germany orchestrated by Loki. The evil god of mischief was disguised as a wolf in sheep's clothing in the form of Abigail's charismatic professor. Under the guidance of Freya, the Norse god of beauty, Abigail learned to find her voice, and her supersonic vocal powers to wield her mythic weapon to stop Evil in its tracks.

Using their powers and strengths, these teenagers might just have what it takes to be the new Gods of today. Now, meet the next three adolescents that, along with Yuko, Amir, and Abigail, may be Earth's

...AND A WEEK AGO THIS CEREMONY MARKED THE CONCLUSION OF A FORMIDABLE ODYSSEY. THAT WHICH BROUGHT A TEAM OF ASTRONAUTS TO MARS ON BOARD THE "KIRARIN" VESSEL FROM THE JAPANESE SPACE AGENCY, THE *JAXA*...

THESE COURAGEOUS PIONEERS LIVED IN THE VACUUM OF SPACE DURING ALMOST A YEAR AND A HALF, THE TIME OF A ROUND TRIP VOYAGE...

THEY ESTABLISHED A BASE ON MARS FROM WHICH THEY CONDUCTED MULTIPLE EXPEDITIONS TO EXPLORE THE MYSTERIES OF THE RED PLANET...

THIS SUCCESS WAS ONLY POSSIBLE WITH THE PARTICIPATION AND THE SUPPORT OF NUMEROUS BUSINESSES AND LEADING FIGURES WORLDWIDE...

THE CEREMONY WAS TROUBLED, HOWEVER, BY THE ABRUPT SICKNESS OF ASTRONAUT *SAKURAKO ABE*...

THERE! THAT'S *MRS. FOURCHON!* SHE IS SO BEAUTIFUL, SO INTELLIGENT.

DID YOU KNOW THAT MRS. FOURCHON IS ONE OF THE MOST BRILLIANT RESEARCHERS OF CONTAGIOUS DISEASES? SHE IS EVEN AUTHORIZED TO WORK IN A P4 LABORATORY.

P4?

A LABORATORY THAT HANDLES CLASS 4 PATHOGENS, THE MOST DANGEROUS VIRUSES IN THE WORLD.

BUT THE MOST FABULOUS PART IS THAT MRS. FOURCHON IS ALSO THE PRESIDENT OF THE *NGO** FOR WHICH I VOLUNTEER.

AH, IF I COULD ONLY MEET HER IN REAL LIFE... WHEN I AM AN ADULT, I WOULD LIKE TO BE JUST LIKE HER.

...LET'S MOVE ON NOW TO THAT MYSTERIOUS SICKNESS THAT THE DOCTORS ARE CALLING "SUPER RAGE." THIS SICKNESS APPEARED THREE DAYS AGO AND IS SPREADING PRINCIPALLY IN THE POOR DISTRICTS OF OUR BIG CITIES. WITNESSES SAY THAT THE VICTIMS ACT LIKE THEY ARE POSSESSED AND CRAZY...

FOR THE MOMENT, THERE ISN'T A TREATMENT AND THE AUTHORITIES ARE OBLIGED TO CONFINE THESE POOR PEOPLE TO CELLS IN ORDER TO TRY TO CONTAIN WHAT LOOKS TO BECOME AN EPIDEMIC.

Breaking NEWS

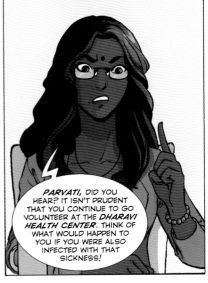

PARVATI, DID YOU HEAR? IT ISN'T PRUDENT THAT YOU CONTINUE TO GO VOLUNTEER AT THE *DHARAVI HEALTH CENTER*. THINK OF WHAT WOULD HAPPEN TO YOU IF YOU WERE ALSO INFECTED WITH THAT SICKNESS!

*NON-GOVERNMENTAL ORGANIZATION

I WILL BE CAREFUL, MA, DON'T WORRY. BUT I AM COMMITTED TO HELPING OUT AT THE FREE CLINIC, AND I CAN'T GO BACK ON MY WORD.

WHEN I BECOME A GREAT LAWYER, I WILL BE ABLE TO HELP ALL THE OPPRESSED.

YOU'RE OVERDOING IT, MY DAUGHTER, YOU ARE STILL YOUNG, TAKE TIME TO HAVE FUN.

IT'LL WORK OUT. I HAVE ENOUGH ENERGY TO DO MY STUDIES AND SAVE THE WORLD. BUT I MUST RUN SO I'M NOT LATE FOR SCHOOL!

DON'T FORGET THAT TOMORROW YOU HAVE A FIELD TRIP TO THE ZOO.

EVERYTHING IS NOTED IN MY CALENDAR, MA!

YOU WERE INCREDIBLE DURING THE MATCH, PARVATI!

IT LOOKED LIKE YOU HAD TEN ARMS TO CATCH ALL THE BALLS LIKE YOU DID.

PARVATI, WE ARE GOING TO HANG OUT AT THE MALL. WOULD YOU LIKE TO JOIN US?

YES, COME RELAX A LITTLE WITH US. YOU'RE ALWAYS DOING TEN THOUSAND THINGS AT A TIME. I REALLY DON'T KNOW HOW YOU FIND THE ENERGY.

THANKS, *MANALI,* BUT I CAN'T. I HAVE TO GO HELP AT THE HEALTH CENTER. THE SCHOOL NURSE, *ANJALI,* GAVE ME A PACKAGE OF COMPRESSES FOR THE SICK.

COME ON, GRAMPS! WE KNOW THAT YOU PICKED UP SOME MONEY.

GIVE IT TO US WITHOUT ANY EXCUSES. WE DON'T WANT TO DIRTY OURSELVES BEATING YOU UP.

HAVE PITY, PLEASE! IF I GIVE IT TO YOU, I WON'T HAVE ANYTHING TO BUY FOOD...

THERE WE ARE, IT'S NOTHING SERIOUS. IT WILL GET BETTER QUICKLY IF YOU REST.

THANK YOU, MY DEAR PARVATI. YOU ARE ALWAYS THERE TO HELP US.

OH, NO, I DON'T DO ANYTHING BUT TEND TO LITTLE BOO-BOOS, IT'S THE DOCTORS LIKE *RAHUL* WHO TAKE CARE OF THE TRULY SICK.

ARE YOU TALKING ABOUT ME? I'M HAPPY TO SEE YOU, PARVATI.

RAHUL! HOW DID THE OPERATION GO?

EVERYTHING WENT WELL, BUT TELL ME, HOW ARE YOUR PARENTS? IT'S BEEN AN ETERNITY SINCE I SPENT AN EVENING PLAYING POKER WITH YOUR FATHER.

WELL, LOOKIE HERE! DID YOU GET A TATTOO ON YOUR ARM?

WHAT? NO, OF COURSE NOT! MY PARENTS WOULD NEVER PERMIT IT.

HOW DID THAT GET THERE?! WITH ALL THAT I'VE HAD TO DO THESE LAST FEW DAYS, BETWEEN MY EVENING CLASSES AND THE TIME I ACCOMPANIED THAT LOST CHILD TO THE POLICE STATION WHILE PASSING BY--

IT'S NOT SERIOUS, PARVATI, IT'S NOT MY BUSINESS ANYWAY. COME, I HAVE A SURPRISE FOR YOU.

EXCUSE ME, MRS. FOURCHON, I PRESENT TO YOU THE SHINING STAR OF OUR VOLUNTEERS: PARVATI PATEL.

PLEASED TO MEET YOU, MISS PATEL.

NAMASTE*! IT'S REALLY YOU! MRS. FOURCHON, I AM YOUR GREATEST ADMIRER. TO BE ABLE TO MEET YOU WAS ONE OF MY DREAMS. BY WHAT MIRACLE IS THIS POSSIBLE?

UH, WELL, THE NGO THAT I CHAIR SPONSORS A GREAT PART OF THIS LITTLE CLINIC DIRECTED MASTERFULLY BY RAHUL.

WHEN I CAN, I LIKE TO MEET THE FOOT SOLDIERS AND TO BE ABLE TO OBSERVE THE RESULTS THAT THEY ARE ACHIEVING. SO, NATURALLY, HERE I AM TODAY.

THAT'S TERRIFIC! THANKS TO YOU, WE ARE ABLE TO HELP PEOPLE HERE.

NO, IT'S THANKS TO YOU! I AM TRULY HAPPY TO SEE THAT THERE ARE YOUNG GIRLS LIKE YOU WHO ARE FULL OF LIFE AND WHO MAKE SURE THAT THE WORLD BECOMES MORE BEAUTIFUL AND MORE JUST.

COUNT ON ME, I WILL REDOUBLE EFFORTS!

FOR THAT, IT WOULD BE NECESSARY FOR YOU TO DOUBLE YOURSELF! YOU'RE ALREADY DOING SO MUCH!

RIGHT NOW? I'M WORKING ON THE VACCINE THAT WOULD SAVE PEOPLE FROM THE MYSTERIOUS SICKNESS THAT IS DRIVING PEOPLE CRAZY. MY TEAM AND I SHOULDN'T TAKE LONG TO FIND THE RIGHT DOSAGE. I AM CERTAIN THAT I WILL COME BACK TO THE CLINIC SOON TO GIVE YOU THE VACCINES.

HA HA HA HA HA HA HA!!

PARDON MY INDISCRETION, MRS. FOURCHON, BUT I'M DYING TO KNOW WHAT YOU'RE WORKING ON RIGHT NOW.

YOU ARE TRULY TERRIFIC!

*"HELLO" IN HINDI.

16

TELL ME, PARVATI, WHAT DOES THIS SCARF TIED TO YOUR ARM SIGNIFY?

UH... IT'S TO REMIND ME OF MY DAY YESTERDAY!

ARE YOU AWARE, ANJALI, THAT I WAS ABLE TO SPEAK WITH MRS. FOURCHON? SHE IS AN EXCEPTIONAL SCIENTIST AND SHE IS WORKING ON THE VACCINE THAT WILL CONTAIN "THE SUPER-RAGE."

I TRULY HOPE THAT SHE WILL FIND THIS REMEDY. THE PEOPLE TOUCHED BY THIS SICKNESS LOSE ALL SENSE OF REALITY AND BECOME VERY VIOLENT.

I AM CERTAIN THAT SHE WILL DO IT! BUT RIGHT NOW, I AM PARTICULARLY IMPATIENT TO SEE THE TWO BABY TIGERS AT THIS ZOO. THEY SEEM SO ADORABLE.

IS IT SAFE FOR THE CHILDREN TO APPROACH THE TIGERS?

DON'T WORRY YOURSELF, MISS, THE ENCLOSURES ARE PERFECTLY SECURE. AND JUST IN ANY CASE, A LITTLE SHOT OF MY SEDATIVE DART AND THE UNCOOPERATIVE BEAST WILL SLEEP LIKE A FAT TOMCAT.

THE LITTLE ONES ARE REALLY TOO CUTE! MAKES ME WANT TO CUDDLE THEM.

I DON'T RECOMMEND IT! MAMA TIGERS ARE VERY PROTECTIVE. TIGERS WEIGH OVER THREE HUNDRED POUNDS. JUST IMAGINE WHAT HAPPENS WHEN THEY CHARGE YOU.

WATCH OUT, PARVATI!

ANJALI?!

OH, NO! SHE LOST CONSCIOUSNESS.

WELL, I DID VERY MUCH WANT TO SEE YOU CLOSE UP, BUT NOW, YOU'RE A LITTLE *TOO* CLOSE.

CRAR

UUUUHHH... UAAAASH...

AIYO,* THIS ISN'T REAL! LISTEN TO ME, WE CAN HELP YOU, BUT YOU MUST CALM YOURSELVES...

*"DARN" IN HINDI.

I DON'T WANT TO END EATEN BY A TIGER NOR TRANSFORMED INTO AN ANGRY ZOMBIE! I WANT TO BECOME A GREAT LAWYER, YOU HEAR ME?!

YOU SHOULDN'T BE AFRAID OF TIGERS...

WHO-- WHO IS TALKING TO ME?

THIS ISN'T REAL! I THINK IT'S TOO LATE. I MUST ALREADY BE INFECTED WITH THE VIRUS!

YOU ARE NOT SICK, YOUNG GIRL, YOU HAVE BEEN CHOSEN. YOU HAVE RECEIVED POWERS, AMONG THEM THE POWER TO TAME TIGERS.

WHAT? I WILL NEVER BE ABLE TO SUBDUE THEM! I AM NOTHING BUT A SIMPLE SCHOOLKID! I AM GOING TO DISAPPEAR BEFORE ACCOMPLISHING MY DESTINY!

GET A HOLD OF YOURSELF! YOU CAN SAVE YOURSELF AND YOUR FRIEND AS WELL.

I-- IF I SHOULD DIE, AT LEAST I WILL HELP FEED THE BABY TIGERS.

THE TIGER ACCEPTS YOU AS AN EQUAL!

...

THANK YOU, MY FRIEND!

HERE'S THE PERFECT WAY TO CALM THE SICK AND TO SAVE THE HEALTHY PEOPLE!

USE THE TIGER AS A MOUNT! HE IS ROBUST AND FAST!

EXCELLENT ADVICE! *LET'S GO!*

I WAS A LITTLE OPTIMISTIC IN THINKING THAT WE COULD FIX THE PROBLEM WITH JUST A LITTLE TRANQUILIZER GUN. I WOULD NEED AT LEAST TEN ARMS TO OVERCOME THESE SICK PEOPLE.

INCREDIBLE! THAT WORKS!

I'M STILL COUNTING ON YOU, MY FRIEND!

PRECISELY, YOU DO HAVE TEN ARMS! ALL YOU HAVE TO DO IS THINK OF ALL THAT YOU WANT TO DO FOR THEM TO BE THERE!

VAAARR...

UGH!

THK

THK

EEEGH...

TCHK

THK

THK

THK

THEY ARE ALL SLEEPING PEACEFULLY. WE DID GREAT WORK.

THE MEDICAL TEAMS ARE ARRIVING.

WEEEEOOO.. WEEEEE OOO.. WEE

THANKS! WITHOUT A DOUBT, I WOULD NOT HAVE SURVIVED WITHOUT YOU AND I CERTAINLY WOULDN'T HAVE BEEN ABLE TO SAVE ALL THOSE PEOPLE. I AM HAPPY TO HAVE FOUND SUCH A FRIEND... BUT I AM OBLIGED TO LEAVE YOU AT THE ZOO.

NO, YOU CAN KEEP HIM WITH YOU. I ALSO HAD A TIGER AT MY SIDE; HE WAS CALLED DAMON. HE WAS MY MOST LOYAL COMPANION.

MAYBE THAT WAS POSSIBLE IN YOUR DAY, BUT HE TAKES UP TOO MUCH SPACE FOR ME TO GET HIM DISCREETLY INTO MY HOUSE. AND I DOUBT THAT THE ZOOKEEPERS WILL LET ME TAKE HIM.

USE YOUR POWER. YOU CAN GIVE HIM ANOTHER APPEARANCE, LET'S SAY, ONE MORE PRACTICAL TO CARRY! CONCENTRATE ON THIS IMAGE...

MEON!

PURR..

OH? GREAT! I'M GOING TO CALL YOU SHAHRUK!

PARVATI, YOU ARE HEALTHY AND SAFE! WHAT HAPPENED?

EVERYTHING IS GREAT, ANJALI. THE INFECTED PEOPLE WERE KNOCKED OUT BY THE GUARD THANKS TO HIS TRANQUILIZER GUN.

JUST ONE GUARD? WITH A SINGLE GUN FOR SO MANY PEOPLE?!...

WE NEED YOU TO EVACUATE THE AREA, PLEASE.

IT'S ME, MA.

MY DARLING, BUT...WHAT ARE YOU DOING WITH THAT CAT?

UH... I FOUND HIM WITH ANJALI, THE SCHOOL NURSE. HE IS IN PERFECT HEALTH AND DOESN'T HAVE ANY FLEAS! PLEASE, MA, I WOULD LIKE TO KEEP HIM.

HMM... WELL, YOUNG LADY. HE'S AN ANIMAL, AND NOT A TOY. YOU WILL BE THE ONLY ONE RESPONSIBLE FOR HIM. YOU MUST TAKE CARE OF HIM, FEED HIM, CHANGE HIS LITTER, AND GIVE HIM YOUR TIME AND YOUR AFFECTION. DO YOU THINK YOU ARE CAPABLE OF THAT?

YES! I SWEAR I WILL, YOUR HONOR!

WHAT ARE ALL THESE FILES, MA?

THE POLICE RECEIVED A NUMBER OF REPORTS OF DISAPPEARANCES IN THE REGION. THEY CAME TO ASK FOR THE HELP OF THE TRIBUNAL PERSONNEL TO ADVANCE THE INVESTIGATION. BUT FOR THE MOMENT, WE'RE FINDING NOTHING.

COME ON, ENOUGH WORK! COME HELP ME PREPARE A GOOD DINNER. YOU FATHER WILL GET BACK LATE FROM THE MINISTRY. TONIGHT, LET'S MAKE HIM A SURPRISE.

...THESE POWERS SEEM VERY PRACTICAL, BUT I WOULD VERY MUCH LIKE TO UNDERSTAND HOW THEY CAME TO ME.

AND YOU'RE TELLING ME THAT IT HAS SOMETHING TO DO WITH THIS TATTOO?

I AM *DURGA* AND YOU ARE MY DESCENDANT. THE TATTOO IS THE MARK OF THE HERO. IF IT APPEARS, IT MEANS THAT EVIL HAS COME BACK TO THE EARTH.

FROM WHAT INFORMATION I HAVE FOUND, YOU ARE ONE OF OUR MAJOR DEITIES. YOU BATTLED NUMEROUS DEMONS. YOU ARE THE POSSESSOR OF THE TEN SACRED WEAPONS... AND YOU EVEN HAVE A FESTIVAL IN YOUR HONOR, IN CALCUTTA AND IN BENGAL!

OH, MOTHER OF THE WORLD, I AM HONORED TO BE YOUR DESCENDANT.

I AM JUST AS HONORED AS YOU, PARVATI! DESTINY COULDN'T HAVE CHOSEN BETTER THAN A YOUNG GIRL SUCH AS YOURSELF: DARING, STRONG, AND INTELLIGENT.

I AM READY TO FIGHT THIS EVIL. TELL ME WHAT I MUST DO.

BEFORE THAT, IT'S NECESSARY THAT YOU GET ME OUT OF THE SPIRIT WORLD. GIVE ME A LITTLE OF YOUR ENERGY SO THAT I CAN MATERIALIZE MYSELF INTO THE REAL WORLD.

OPEN YOUR HEART AND THE GIFT WILL GIVE ITSELF.

YOU ARE TOO CUTE LIKE THAT!

NAMASTE, SHAHRUK!

? POOF

AH, BUT YES, I AM BRILLIANT! IS IT POSSIBLE TO BE SO INTELLIGENT? WITHOUT MY SUPERIOR MIND, YOU WOULD TRULY SERVE NO PURPOSE.

OH, SUPREME MISTRESS, WE WOULD NEED A DEMONIC FORCE TO ACHIEVE YOUR PLAN.

I AM GOING TO UNITE DEMONIC NATURE AND MODERN SCIENCE TO PLUNGE HUMANITY INTO CHAOS AND DESTRUCTION. I KEEP THE COMPANY OF JADIS, A DEMON WHO DISFIGURED A GODDESS. HE WILL HANDLE THINGS PERFECTLY.

AS FOR YOU, MISERABLE LARVA, MAKE YOURSELVES USEFUL! GO LOOK FOR OTHER GUINEA PIGS, WHILE I TAKE CARE OF MY DEMON.

BUT ENOUGH WASTING TIME WITH YOU, I MUST SAY HELLO TO MY OLD FRIEND!

LEAVE THESE PEOPLE ALONE!

GRR RRAOO!

A TIGER?!

24

BLENG

POC

CRASH CLONK

IS IT OVER?

LET'S TAKE THIS AS A CHANCE TO FLEE WITH AS MANY PEOPLE AS POSSIBLE!

STOP! GET BACK HERE!

NO! WHY DID MY POWER STOP WORKING?

I'M SORRY ABOUT YOUR FRIENDS, PARVATI! WHAT HAPPENED IS DUE TO THE FACT THAT YOU DON'T YET HAVE FULL POSSESSION OF YOUR POWERS. YOU NEED THE LEGENDARY WEAPONS TO TAP ENTIRELY INTO THE ENERGY THAT IS IN YOU.

I NEED TO FIND RAHUL AND FREE ALL THE PEOPLE WHO WERE TAKEN.

SO, LET'S GO LOOK FOR THE WEAPONS RIGHT AWAY! I LEFT THEM IN A GROTTO WELL HIDDEN FROM ANYONE'S VIEW.

NOOOOO! IT'S NOT POSSIBLE!

WHAT? WHAT IS IT?

INDIAN EX

NATION · WORLD · STATES · CITIES · BUSINESS · SPORT · ENTERTAINMENT · GALLERIES · VIDEOS

Home › Nation

Illegal Extraction Of $1,000 Goa

AT THE SPOT WHERE YOUR GROTTO WAS, TODAY THERE ARE ONLY THE REMAINS OF AN IRON ORE QUARRY.

I DON'T QUITE UNDERSTAND...

WELL, UH, THERE IS NO LONGER A GROTTO AND SO, THERE ARE NO WEAPONS. HOW ARE WE GOING TO SAVE EVERYONE NOW?

PARVATI? IS EVERYTHING OKAY?

NO, IT'S NOT, ANJALI. I WAS RESEARCHING RELICS THAT SHOULD HAVE BEEN ON THE SITE OF THAT QUARRY--

WAIT, I KNOW THIS PLACE...

THE ARCHEOLOGICAL OBJECTS THAT WERE DISCOVERED HERE WERE TAKEN TO *CHHATRAPATI SHIVAJI MAHARAJ VASTU SANGRAHALAYA*, THE MUMBAI MUSEUM OF HISTORY AND ART. I THINK THAT THEY ARE STILL EXHIBITED THERE TODAY.

THANKS, ANJALI!

YOU SAVED OUR LIVES!

LITERALLY, WITHOUT THE WEAPONS, WE WERE DEAD! WELL, AT LEAST YOU... ME, I AM ALREADY!

...

HERE'S THE MUSEUM!

IT'S IMMENSE HERE! WHERE HAVE THEY PUT THE ANCIENT RELICS?!

DURGA, WHAT DO THESE WEAPONS LOOK LIKE?

LIKE THAT! THANKFULLY, THEY ARE HERE. AND INTACT.

YOU CAN TAKE THE WEAPON!

WELL, ALL OF THEM! LOOK, YOU ONLY HAVE TO--

UH... WHICH DO YOU MEAN? THERE ARE TEN OF THEM.

BRAAAOOM

CRRRRR

PERFECT! EXACTLY IN THE RIGHT SPOT! I'M NEVER MISTAKEN, ISN'T IT FANTASTIC?!

HA HA HA

MAMA, THERE'S A BLUE MONSTER!

HELP!

COME ON!

DON'T MOVE! UH... MONSTER?

WE WON'T HESITATE TO FIRE AT YOU... SO, HANDS... ALL FOUR HANDS UP!

YOUR PRESENCE OFFENDS MY VIEW, YOU MISERABLE INSECTS! DISAPPEAR!

SCHBAFF

KALI! SO, EVIL HAS EMBODIED THIS ODIOUS CREATURE! PARVATI, HERE IS WHAT YOU MUST BATTLE AND DESTROY! TAKE THE STATUE'S DISK!

PERFECT! AT LEAST, WE WON'T HAVE TO LOOK FOR HER! LET'S GET TO WORK!

WHAT?! THIS LITTLE MOSQUITO IS THE NEW PROTECTOR OF "GOOD"? POOR LITTLE GIRL, YOU CAN'T POSSIBLY OPPOSE MY PERFECTION! AND YOU WON'T EVEN HAVE THE CHANCE TO APPRECIATE MY SUBLIME INTELLIGENCE BECAUSE YOU WILL BE DEAD BEFORE YOU CAN COUNT TO TEN!

TCHOCK

CALL TO THE SACRED WEAPONS!

SACRED WEAPONS!

POC

OH, NO! SHAHRUK!

MIOUW

SEE HOW YOU UNRAVEL? I DON'T KNOW WHY I'M BOTHERING! A FEW UNDERLINGS SHOULD SUFFICE TO RID ME OF YOU!

YOU MUST NOT LOSE COURAGE. YOU HAVE COMPLICATED WEAPONS TO USE AND YOU HAVEN'T HAD THE TIME TO TRAIN WITH THEM.

BUT, DURGA, I COMPLETELY MISSED THE CHANCE TO FIGHT KALI! I DID NOTHING OF IMPORTANCE!

IT'LL COME TO YOU. YOU MUST LEARN THE POWERS OF EACH ONE. AND DON'T FORGET THAT YOU ALSO HAVE TEN ARMS!

TEN ARMS...? BUT YOU'RE RIGHT. I SHOULD STOP LAMENTING!

SO THAT'S HOW IT IS, KALI USES INNOCENTS TO FIGHT IN HER PLACE?

YES, AND AS FAR AS THAT IS CONCERNED, I DON'T KNOW IF YOU NOTICED, BUT THE BEHAVIOR OF THE PEOPLE THAT SHE BEWITCHED GREATLY RESEMBLES THAT OF THE SICK PEOPLE AT THE ZOO.

ALL OF THESE WOUNDED... I COULDN'T DO ANYTHING, I'M USELESS... AND YOU, MY POOR SHAHRUK...

PARVATI, DON'T SAY THAT. IT'S YOU WHO SHATTERED THE RUINS WITH THAT MALLET. WITHOUT WHICH, THESE PEOPLE WOULD HAVE BEEN KILLED!

OH, YEAH! KALI IS CERTAINLY AT THE ORIGIN OF THE SICKNESS!

WHERE ARE YOU GOING?

IF THE GODDESS WANTS TO SPREAD THE DISEASE, THOSE WHO ARE TRYING TO CURE IT WILL BE HER ENEMIES. MRS. FOURCHON IS TRYING TO DEVELOP A VACCINE. I MUST WARN HER THAT SHE IS IN DANGER!

WHAT NOW?

IF IT'S THE SUPER-RAGE, WHAT WE DID AT THE ZOO COULD WORK AGAIN! IT'S NECESSARY TO FIND THE WAY TO KNOCK OUT THE SICK PEOPLE WITHOUT HURTING THEM. I'M GOING TO TALK TO ANJALI ABOUT IT.

THAT'S THE PARVATI I LOVE! YOU CAN DO IT!

TIME IS RUNNING OUT! THERE ARE MORE AND MORE SICK PEOPLE! I HOPE THAT RAHUL IS OKAY!

PARVATI, THANK YOU FOR COMING OUT TO WARN ME.

I HEARD WHAT HAPPENED AT THE FREE CLINIC, AND I AM PROFOUNDLY SORRY FOR WHAT HAPPENED TO THE VOLUNTEER TEAM, ESPECIALLY BECAUSE THESE PEOPLE GIVE THEIR LIVES TO HELP OTHERS.

EXCUSE MY CURIOSITY, MRS. FOURCHON, BUT WHAT'S IN THESE SYRINGES?

THIS IS OUR GREATEST HOPE! MY TEAM AND I HAVE JUST FINISHED DEVELOPING A VACCINE. WE THINK THAT IT WILL BE EFFECTIVE. THE AUTHORITIES ARE GOING TO BE IN CHARGE OF ADMINISTERING THEM.

PARVATI, THERE'S NOTHING ELSE FOR YOU TO DO. ALL WILL BE WELL NOW.

THANK YOU FOR TAKING THE TIME TO LISTEN TO ME.

PARVATI, I JUST THOUGHT I SAW--

NOT NOW, I MUST HURRY TO SEE ANJALI BEFORE I HEAD HOME. IT'S ALREADY LATE AND MY PARENTS MUST BE WORRIED! AND TONIGHT, YOU WILL TEACH ME TO USE THE WEAPONS!

34

THE NEXT MORNING...

IT'S BETTER THAN BECOMING ONE OF THOSE NUTCASES WHO BREAK EVERYTHING, RIGHT?

⹂BRRR!⹂ I'M SCARED OF SHOTS! I ONLY HAVE TO THINK OF THEM, AND I GET WEAK IN THE KNEES.

ME, I'M SICK OF WAITING, IT MUST BE THREE HOURS THAT WE'VE BEEN STANDING AROUND.

IT'S OKAY, IT'LL SOON BE OUR TURN.

HOW DO YOU LOOK SO GOOD AFTER SPENDING THE NIGHT BRANDISHING WEAPONS?!

YOU WRITE YOUR NAME, YOUR AGE, YOUR ADDRESS, AND THE NAME OF YOUR PARENTS, PLEASE.

PARVATI PA--

JUST A SEC!

PARVATI, COME WITH ME, I NEED TO TALK WITH YOU!

BUT-- IT'S MY TURN TO RECEIVE THE VACCINE...

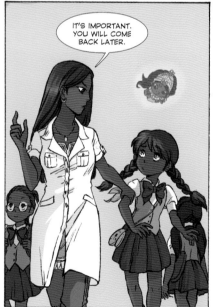

IT'S IMPORTANT. YOU WILL COME BACK LATER.

LISTEN TO ME! IT'S NOT A GOOD IDEA TO GET THIS VACCINE. THIS TREATMENT HAS BEEN DEVELOPED IN HASTE, WE HAVEN'T TAKEN THE TIME TO TRULY VERIFY ITS EFFECTS.

WE MUST BE PRUDENT WITH THE SUBSTANCES THAT WE INJECT IN OUR BODIES. ONCE WE PUT SOMETHING THERE, IT CAN'T BE UNDONE!

BUT MRS. FOURCHON IS A GENIUS BIOLOGIST! SHE HAS ALREADY CONTRIBUTED NUMEROUS MEDICAL ADVANCES!

THIS MAKES NO SENSE! IF KALI TRULY IS CAUSING ALL THIS INSANITY, SHE SHOULD HAVE INTERVENED TODAY AND STOPPED THE TRUCKS DISTRIBUTING THE ANTIDOTES.

INSTEAD, THOUSANDS OF PEOPLE WERE VACCINATED AND THEY ARE ALL SLEEPING PEACEFULLY IN THEIR HOMES. AND OUR SURVEILLANCE OF THE LABORATORY HAS NOT GIVEN US ANYTHING EITHER.

I HAVEN'T EVEN SEEN MRS. FOURCHON. AND I HAVEN'T PROGRESSED AN IOTA IN MY INVESTIGATION OF THE ABDUCTION OF THE VOLUNTEERS.

I ONLY SEE TWO POSSIBLE EXPLANATIONS: EITHER KALI ISN'T THE SOURCE OF THE SICKNESS, OR, QUITE THE OPPOSITE, SHE HOPES THAT EVERYONE GETS THE VACCINE AND--

WHAT WAS THAT SOUND?! A... A CRATE OF MANGOES??

...

STAY HERE.

OH, BRAHMA... THE VIRUS HAS SPREAD DESPITE THE VACCINATION!

MAKE SURE ALL THE DOORS AND WINDOWS ARE PROPERLY LOCKED!

PANIC HAS OVERRUN MOST OF THE DISTRICTS WEST OF THE CITY. THE MAIN PROBLEM IS THAT THE LAW ENFORCEMENT SERVICES THEMSELVES HAVE FALLEN PREY TO THE SYMPTOMS OF THE SICKNESS!

FOR THE MOMENT, THE AUTHORITIES ADVISE EVERYONE TO STAY AT HOME. HERE'S THE LIST OF INSTRUCTIONS TO CARRY OUT--

I MUST ACT!

LET'S GO HELP THESE POOR PEOPLE!

45

THE SITUATION IS EVEN WORSE THAN BEFORE.

BUT IT'S MANALI AND *TRIPTA!* THEY WERE VACCINATED THIS MORNING?!

YES, BEFORE ANJALI STOPPED YOU! SOMETHING IS WRONG WITH THE VACCINE! THAT'S WHY KALI DIDN'T INTERVENE!

OF COURSE! KALI INFECTED MRS. FOURCHON'S VACCINE. WE MUST GO TO THE LABORATORY. SHE MAY BE IN DANGER!

LIGHTNING BOLT OF INDRA!

SCHBOM

WELL, NOW IT'S A QUESTION OF HOW TO GET IN! IT'S AN ABSOLUTE FORTRESS.

USE THE LIGHTNING BOLT OF INDRA. THAT WEAPON CAN DESTROY ANY OBSTACLE.

NOW INVOKE THE SOLAR DISK OF VISHNU.

SOLAR DISK OF VISHNU!

IT SEEMS COMPLETELY DESERTED. NOT EVEN A GUARD. IT'S VERY STRANGE.

GRRRR

WHAT IS IT, SHAHRUK?

IT'S ONLY A STATUE...

OF KALI! WHY PUT AN EFFIGY OF THE GODDESS OF DESTRUCTION IN A PLACE WHERE PEOPLE ARE CURED?

IT'S WEIRD... THE EYES ARE ODDLY TWO DIFFERENT COLORS...

CRRR

A SECRET PASSAGE! WELL DONE, PARVATI!

PARVATI, I THINK THAT THERE IS NO LONGER ANY DOUBT THAT MRS. FOURCHON WORKS FOR KALI!

I NEED TO FIND OUT FOR SURE.

LOOKIE HERE, OUR MOSQUITO IS BACK! I THOUGHT THAT A DOSE OF VACCINE WOULD HAVE TAKEN CARE OF YOU.

HOW COULD YOU? YOU WERE MY HERO. WHY ARE YOU SERVING KALI?!

YOU ARE COMPLETELY MISTAKEN, PARVATI. I DON'T SERVE KALI...

I AM KALI! I AM THE INCARNATION OF EVIL.

OH, OF COURSE, THAT POOR MRS. FOURCHON PUT UP LITTLE RESISTANCE WHEN I CHOSE HER AS HOST.

BUT I HAD NEED OF HER SCIENTIFIC KNOWLEDGE TO DEVELOP THIS VIRUS WHICH WILL SOON REDUCE MAN TO HIS BESTIAL, DEVASTATING INSTINCTS!

MONSTER!

WRETCH!

YOU ALSO HAVE A GREAT BLADE.

AXE OF WISHWAKARMA!

WHERE-- WHERE?...

YOU ARE AT THE HOSPITAL. I BROUGHT YOU HERE FROM THE UNDERGROUND TEMPLE.

AH, YES, THE TEMPLE. AND MRS. FOURCHON?

SHE WAS ARRESTED AND ADMITTED HAVING DEALT OUT VACCINES TO SPREAD THE VIRUS ON A GRAND SCALE. SHE VOWED, HOWEVER, THAT SHE WANTED TO FIX HER MISTAKES BY PROMISING AN EFFECTIVE REMEDY AS SOON AS POSSIBLE.

FOR THAT MATTER, THE MEMBERS OF THE SECT WERE ALL ARRESTED AS WELL. ON THE OTHER HAND, THE POLICE DIDN'T WANT TO BELIEVE ME WHEN I TOLD THEM THAT THE GODDESS KALI HAD TAKEN POSSESSION OF THE SCIENTIST. THEY SAID THAT I WAS DELIRIOUS BECAUSE OF THE VIRUS!

PARVATI!

MY DARLING, WE WERE SO WORRIED FOR YOU!

WHY DID YOU DISAPPEAR LIKE THAT WHEN IT WAS SO DANGEROUS OUTSIDE?

I WANTED TO HELP MY FRIENDS.

BUT ALL IS WELL NOW! THERE IS NO MORE EVIL.

I THINK YOU ARE MISTAKEN, PARVATI... THE MARK IS STILL THERE, IT'S THE SIGN THAT EVIL IS STILL PRESENT, WITHOUT A DOUBT IT HAS JUST CHANGED FORM.

46

NOW IT IS TIME THAT I TALK WITH YOU ABOUT THE OTHER CHOSEN ONES, THE OTHER HEROES... BECAUSE YOU ARE NOT THE ONLY ONE...

PART 5 : MIGUEL

Script
PATRICK SOBRAL
with help from **FABIEN DALMASSO**

Art and Color by
JÉRÔME ALQUIÉ

RMBLL

DON'T LOSE YOUR BALANCE, MIGUEL!

SWWEE

DON'T DO IT FOR ME. I WILL BE THE FIRST TO REACH THE OLD *BRUJA'S** HOUSE!

BELIEVE WHATEVER YOU WANT... BUT I'M GOING TO WIN!

...AND THE SOUTH ZONE WILL BELONG TO THE COBRAS FOR A MONTH!

BUT WHAT IS THAT RUCKUS?

IT'S COMING FROM THE ROOFS!

HEY?! NO, BUT THAT'S NOT RIGHT?!

VLAM

IT'S THOSE KIDS... THE LOBOS AND THE COBRAS... WHO HAVE STARTED SOME KIND OF STUPID CHALLENGE.

SOMEONE SHOULD CALL THE POLICE!

ϡPFFF!ϟ... IT'S BEEN A LONG TIME SINCE THE COPS CAME BY HERE. WHO CARES ABOUT THE INHABITANTS OF THE SLUMS?!

DEPENDS WHO AND WHY!

*SPANISH FOR "WITCH."

I DID--

WHOA...

HA HA HA! I'M TRULY TOO GOOD! I WON! THE LOBOS *WON!*

DID YOU SEE THAT, GUYS?! I--!

OH! HEY, IT'S OKAY, I DON'T STINK THAT BAD, COME ON...

UH-OH...

MIGUEL... I SHOULD HAVE KNOWN...

HELLO, *TIO* ROBERTO!* WASN'T THAT AWESOME?

*SPANISH FOR "UNCLE."

YOU DON'T SMELL GOOD, BIG BROTHER!

YOU SHOULD HAVE MORE CONTROL OVER THE KID, *MARIO.*

IF HE CONTINUES ON THIS PATH, IT'S JUVENILE PRISON WAITING FOR HIM... OR *WORSE!*

POLICÍA

AH, IF ONLY *SARA* WAS STILL AMONG US...

IF YOU DON'T WANT TO GET HIM BACK IN LINE, YOU LEAVE ME NO CHOICE.

GULP

SO EACH DAY AFTER SCHOOL, MIGUEL IS GOING TO VOLUNTEER AT THE *BUENA SUERTE* ASSOCIATION. I'M GOING TO ARRANGE IT. IT MAY TAKE A WHILE, BUT HE WILL LEARN RESPONSIBILITY AND THAT WILL GET HIM OUT OF THE STREET AND AWAY FROM HIS BAD HABITS.

IT'S THAT OR A HOME FOR JUVENILE DELINQUENTS. YOU WILL START TOMORROW AFTER SCHOOL.

SLAM

TIO ROBERTO, LISTEN, YOU DON'T HAVE TO--

* A MARK OF ESTEEM FOR A PERSON OF SOCIAL DISTINCTION.
** SPANISH FOR "THE GIANT."

THE NEXT MORNING...

HUH? WHAT'S THIS...?

I MUST HAVE DONE THAT WHEN I FELL IN THE GARBAGE...

WIPE WIPE

SORRY, THAT WON'T WASH OFF.

NO ONE--

I MUST HAVE PLAYED TOO MUCH "POKE-MONSTER" WITH THE DS THAT I STOLE LAST WEEK...

DIOS*? WHAT?

*SPANISH FOR "GODS."

DON'T WORRY, PAPA, GO BACK TO SLEEP...

IF THE GODS EXIST, WE'D KNOW AND WE WOULDN'T BE IN SUCH A-- ξZZZ!ξ

LET'S GO, LITTLE SISTER, ON OUR WAY!

YESSS! TO SCHOOL, TO SCHOOL!

AND STOP BEING A SMART ALEC JUST BECAUSE YOU WON AT SKATING THE OTHER DAY!

SKATING OR ON A FLYING CARPET, I WILL BRING YOU MISERY WHENEVER YOU WANT!

OH, YEAH?

RIIIP

YEAH.

SCRUNCH

?!

I'M FASTER THAN YOU!

IN YOUR DREAMS!

DON'T BREAK THE RHYTHM, MIGUEL. YOU'VE CAUGHT THE ATTENTION OF THE BIG BOSS.

DON ALVAREZ? REALLY?

DON ALVAREZ, DO YOU WANT ME TO INTERVENE?

RMBLL

VLAM

HEY! INSTEAD OF WATCHING THE SHOW, PAY ATTENTION TO WHAT YOU'RE DOING!

LOOK OUT! THE CRATE!

FRAGILE

CRIIISH

SNAKES?!

SNAKES!

RUN, RUN!

WHAT A BUNCH OF IMBECILES!

CLOSE THE DOORS OF THE WAREHOUSE AND--?!

CLiC CLiC

PUT AWAY YOUR WEAPON, IDIOT! DON'T DARE TO HURT THE MERCHANDISE!

VLAM

ANYONE WHO SHOOTS AT THE SNAKES WILL HAVE TO DEAL WITH ME!

GO, HIT THE ROAD, DIRTY BEASTS!

BRRRR

AHHH! YOU'RE SUCH A MORON, MIGUEL! THAT DIDN'T HELP AT ALL, NOW WE'LL BOTH GET EATEN!

IF WE DO NOTHING, THEN THAT'S SURE TO HAPPEN!

THEY'RE GETTING CLOSER! THEY'RE GETTING CLOSER!

I'M NOT BLIND! I--

SKRAAAAOM

A--A TORNADO?!

LET ME GO, I'M NO BABY!

HEY!

PAF

THAT'S HOW YOU EXPRESS GRATITUDE?!

GET LOST, MIGUEL! I DIDN'T ASK YOU FOR ANYTHING!

CLAP CLAP

BRAVO, KIDS, BRAVO.

CLAP CLAP

UH, WELL, WE COULD SAY THAT LUCK--

WHAT AM I SAYING, LUCK?... IT'S CLEAR THAT THE GODS ARE WITH YOU, BOYS!

THE SNAKES ARE ALL DEAD...

EL GIGANTE IS GOING TO BE FURIOUS.

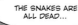

YOU ARE TOO GENEROUS, DON ALVAREZ. BUT... WHY ARE YOU GIVING ME THIS MONEY?

COME ON, IT'S THE LEAST I COULD DO IN RECOMPENSE FOR THIS MISADVENTURE...

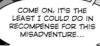

IN FACT, COME SEE ME THE DAY AFTER TOMORROW AT THE WAREHOUSE, AT NOON. I WILL HAVE SOMETHING TO PROPOSE TO YOU.

THE DAY AFTER TOMORROW...

AFTER TOMORROW! BUT THAT'S SUNDAY! ALVAREZ DOESN'T MAKE SENSE...

ANOTHER SNAKE!

GET OUT OF HERE, DIRTY BEAST!

SPLASH

YOUR VIOLENCE IS USELESS. YOU DON'T NEED TO BE AFRAID OF ME. I AM HERE TO HELP YOU.

THE ONLY ONE WHO MIGHT HAVE HELPED ME TODAY IS GOD WHO JUST SENT THE TORNADO TO THE WAREHOUSE.

NO, MY YOUNG FRIEND. YOUR "GOD" DID NOTHING THERE. THAT WAS YOU!

I AM THE SPIRIT OF THE AZTEC GOD *QUETZALCOATL*, THE FEATHERED SERPENT.

YOU ARE MY DESCENDANT, MIGUEL, AND AS I WAS IN MY TIME, YOU ARE THE GUARDIAN OF THE POWER OF WIND.

OH, SURE, RIGHT...

I SAY IT AND I WILL PROVE IT! THAT BANDANA ON YOUR FOREHEAD IS HIDING A MARK THAT SHOWED UP RECENTLY, ISN'T IT?

IT'S THE SIGN THAT EVIL, WHO I BATTLED AND VANQUISHED LONG AGO, IS BACK ON EARTH. AND THAT YOU ARE DESTINED TO BATTLE HIM.

SORRY, "QUETZI," BUT I'M NOT PLANNING ON MOVING FROM THIS SPOT.

IT'S QUETZALCOATL, NOT QUETZI, THANKS. AND IT'S MORE THAN LIKELY THAT EVIL HAS TAKEN POSSESSION OF SOMEONE HERE, MAYBE EVEN ONE OF YOUR CLOSEST FRIENDS, AND IF HE HAS THE CHANCE, HE WILL TRY TO ELIMINATE YOU BEFORE YOUR TRAINING CAN BE ACHIEVED.

MY TRAINING? AS WHAT?

AS A HERO, OF COURSE!

BUENA SUERTE

DO YOU REALLY NEED TO FOLLOW ME EVERYWHERE? SERIOUSLY?

DON'T WORRY, YOU'RE THE ONLY ONE WHO CAN SEE OR HEAR ME, THANKS TO THAT MARK ON YOUR FOREHEAD.

SO JUST ACT LIKE I'M NOT HERE.

THAT'S NOT GOING TO BE EASY.

EXCUSE ME, DON, FOR BEING LATE.

NOC NOC

OH, THERE YOU ARE! COME IN, MIGUEL, WE'VE BEEN WAITING FOR YOU.

WE?

WHAT IS JOAQUIM DOING HERE? YOU'VE TAKEN HIS BLOOD... IS HE SICK?

YOUR FRIEND IS FINE, DON'T WORRY. LET ME EXPLAIN WHY WE ARE HERE, IF I MAY...

AS YOU KNOW, FOR SEVERAL MONTHS, I HAVE BEEN DISTRIBUTING FOOD TO THE POOR IN THE SLUMS OF OUR CITY. BUT I REALIZED THAT I'M ONLY PERPETUATING THEIR HELPLESSNESS IF I CONTINUE IN THIS WAY.

HANDOUT SAYS: NATIONAL BLOOD DONATION CAMPAIGN.

SO THAT PEOPLE UNDERSTAND THE VALUE OF THESE GIFTS, IT'S NECESSARY THAT THOSE BENEFITING CAN GIVE SOMETHING IN RETURN. AND AS THEY DON'T HAVE MONEY...

I DECIDED TO START A MAJOR BLOOD DONATION CAMPAIGN. YOU KNOW HOW BADLY THE HOSPITALS NEED IT.

I SEE. SO, PEOPLE GIVE THEIR BLOOD IN EXCHANGE FOR YOUR DONATIONS, AND IT'S GOOD FOR THE ENTIRE COMMUNITY, THAT'S IT? THAT'S REALLY A GOOD IDEA.

YOU GET IT! YOUR FRIEND JOAQUIM WAS ONE OF THE FIRST TO VOLUNTEER. ISN'T THAT WONDERFUL?

YEAH... EVEN THOUGH THAT SURPRISES ME ABOUT HIM...

I WANT YOU TO DISTRIBUTE THESE HANDOUTS TO PEOPLE IN THE SLUMS. PEOPLE HERE KNOW YOU, THEY WILL BE MORE WILLING TO GIVE THEIR BLOOD. THESE TWO NURSES WILL ACCOMPANY YOU TO COLLECT THE BLOOD.

MOVE IT! CAN'T YOU SEE THAT THEY NEED HELP?!

HELP US!

THERE ARE SURVIVORS UNDERNEATH!

LET'S GO! ALL TOGETHER!

ARRRAAH!

IT'S IMPOSSIBLE TO MOVE!

THERE'S NOTHING WE CAN DO... WE'LL HAVE TO WAIT FOR THE CITY SERVICE VEHICLES TO CLEAR ACCESS...

NO! THE MUD IS STILL COLLECTING AND SEEPING UNDER THE CONCRETE SLAB. BY THE TIME HELP ARRIVES, THE PEOPLE UNDERNEATH WILL BE DEAD AND DROWNED!

MY LITTLE SISTER IS UNDER THERE... PLEASE!

BAM

BAM

BA M

I WON'T LET HER DIE!

MAYAA!

BAAAM

THE SLAB MOVED! BUT OF COURSE, MY POWERS!

MIGUEL, WAKE UP!

⸮SNORFFF.⸮

WHAT'S YOUR PROBLEM WITH PEOPLE WHO ARE SLEEPING, QUETZI?

YAWN

I JUST GOT BACK FROM THE *BUENA SUERTE* WAREHOUSE. I SAW SOME SUSPICIOUS TRUCKS THERE. SOMETHING WEIRD IS GOING ON THERE.

WHAT WERE YOU DOING THERE IN THE MIDDLE OF THE NIGHT?

I HAD A FEELING... AND I WAS RIGHT! I FELT THE SAME WEIRD SENSATION THAT I FELT EARLIER DURING THE DAY.

OKAY, I UNDERSTAND... LET'S GO LOOK MORE CLOSELY.

IS THAT HOW YOU EXPECT TO HELP ME? BY STAYING HIDDEN FROM THE ACTION?

I... I'M JUST BEING CAREFUL, THAT'S ALL. SOMETHING LIKE THIS, IN THE MIDDLE OF THE NIGHT, IT'S DEFINITELY SHADY. THERE ARE RUMORS ABOUT THE TRAFFICKING THAT DON ALVAREZ DOES. IT WOULD BE CRAZY NOT TO SUSPECT THEM.

AND ME, THEY CAN SEE ME. I'M NOT A SPIRIT. I DON'T WANT TO GET MYSELF CAUGHT SPYING.

FEAR DOESN'T SIT WELL WITH THE WARRIOR YOU MUST BECOME.

OH, ARE YOU TRYING TO MAKE MY HEAD EXPLODE?

BUT WITHOUT YOUR POWERS, I WOULDN'T HAVE BEEN ABLE TO SAVE MY SISTER. SO I OWE YOU ONE...

PERFECT, BECAUSE HERE COME SOME PEOPLE!

SKREEE

ALVAREZ!

COME, MY BOY, LET'S NOT LOSE ANY TIME.

JOAQUIM?! WHY IS HE MESSING AROUND HERE?

LOOK AT HIS EYES. HE LOOKS EVEN MORE HAGGARD NOW THAN BEFORE.

LET'S GO.

FOLLOW THEM! GET ON BOARD! GO!

I AM GOING TO HAVE SOME SERIOUS PROBLEMS IF SOMEONE FINDS ME.

SO MAKE SURE THAT DOESN'T HAPPEN.

VROOUM

NONE OF THIS IS GOOD, NOT GOOD AT ALL.

WHAT'S THE PROBLEM? DON'T TELL ME THAT YOU'RE SCARED. I'M THE ONE RISKING THE MOST HERE.

I'M NOT SCARED, I'M WORRIED, YOU NUISANCE!

COME ON, TAKE A BREATH, AND LET ME REMIND YOU THAT YOU WERE THE ONE WHO PUT US IN THIS TRUCK. WHY ARE YOU WORRIED SO MUCH?

THE DIRECTION THAT WE TOOK... IT'S TOWARDS WHERE WE HID THE SERPENT'S TAIL, THE DIVINE WEAPON THAT SHOULD COME BACK TO YOU.

I DON'T SEE ANYONE. YOU CAN GET OUT.

THUMP

AND NOW, WHAT'S HAPPENING? WE'RE MILES FROM THE CITY. IF WE DISAPPEAR HERE, NO ONE WILL EVER FIND US.

LOOK... THAT ENTRANCE WAS RECENTLY DUG.

THAT EXPLAINS ALL THOSE TRUCKS FULL OF DIRT THAT WE SAW PASS US.

WELL, THERE AREN'T THIRTY-SIX WAYS TO FIND OUT WHAT'S AT THE BOTTOM.

YOU IMPRESS ME, MIGUEL. I REALLY THOUGHT THAT YOU WERE GOING TO GIVE UP EARLIER, AND NOW, YOU'RE THE ONE CALLING THE SHOTS, I'M PROUD OF YOU.

DON'T MOCK ME, I AM A BREATH AWAY FROM TURNING BACK ON MY HEELS...

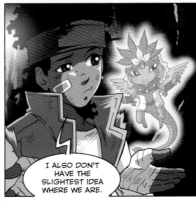

I ALSO DON'T HAVE THE SLIGHTEST IDEA WHERE WE ARE.

THIS WAY! I SENSE SOMETHING. FOLLOW ME!

I'D SAY SOME SORT OF VERY ANCIENT RITUAL SACRIFICE... BUT IT CAN'T BE PRACTICED WITHOUT HUMANS SO...

FLOUSH

THAT'S FROM THE DONATIONS!

LOOK! HOW DID HE GET SO MUCH BLOOD?

NOT FROM A SINGLE CAMPAIGN. HE MUST HAVE DONE HUNDREDS!

ALVAREZ TRICKED US ALL! THAT PIECE OF--

AAAH, BUT IT'S DISGUSTING! WHAT DID HE DO?!

HE'S COMING!

THAT INCANTATION! NO, NO, NO, NO! THAT'S BAD!

LOOK AT THAT HORROR! WE NEED TO GO, QUETZI. LET'S GET OUT OF HERE.

YOU DON'T UNDERSTAND, MIGUEL... EVIL, WHO WE WERE SEARCHING FOR, IS IN THAT MAN. ALVAREZ WAS THE RECEPTACLE!

QUETZI! STEP ON IT!

EVIL TOOK ADVANTAGE OF HIM AND OF HIS FINANCES TO ACCESS THIS PLACE, THE TEMPLE WHERE I CONQUERED HIM CENTURIES AGO BY BEHEADING HIM.

YES, WELL, HE DOESN'T SEEM TO MISS HIS HEAD MUCH! COME ON, WE MUST GET OUT OF HERE.

NOW, THANKS TO THE SACRIFICIAL BLOOD, HE'S TRYING TO REVIVE HIS ORIGINAL BODY, THAT OF *NECOCYAOTL*, THE GOD OF DISSENT AND VIOLENCE!

THAT'S WHO YOU MUST BATTLE!

WOW! CLASSY!

I WON'T LET ANYTHING BAD HAPPEN TO THE MASTER!

HE CHOSE ME AS HIS DEVOTED SERVANT, MY LIFE BELONGS TO HIM!

VLAM

JOAQUIM! STOP THAT! I DON'T WANT TO HURT YOU!

NOO! I WON'T LET YOU, NECOCYAOTL!

MIGUEL, I NEED YOU HERE!

WHY WAS IT THAT I ONLY CAME BACK AS A SPIRIT?!

RROOOWAAAAP?

AAAHHH...

SO I SEE, YOU ARE TRULY THE DESCENDANT OF QUETZALCOATL, MY OLD ENEMY. I SENSED IN YOU THE HIDDEN MAGIC OF THE FEATHERED SNAKE THE FIRST TIME THAT I SAW YOU IN THE WAREHOUSE.

BUT FOR SOME REASON THAT I CAN'T EXPLAIN, THE SAME AURA WAS ALSO AROUND YOUR COMPANION, JOAQUIM. ALL I NEEDED WAS THE MAGIC OF ONE OF YOU, JUST ONE COULD FREE MY SEALED HEAD.

SO I MADE THE TYPE I NEEDED... A DEVOTEE!

YOUR DONATION OF BLOOD! BY GIVING IT, JOAQUIM FOUND HIMSELF A VICTIM OF AN EVIL SPELL.

YOU'VE MADE HIM A SLAVE!

I SEE THAT YOU UNDERSTAND! ALL WHO GAVE ME THEIR BLOOD ARE NOW MY SUBJECTS! I POSSESS AN ARMY READY TO SPREAD DISSENTION THROUGHOUT MEXICO.

THE MORE WOUNDED THERE ARE IN THE BATTLES AT THE HANDS OF MY ARMY, THE MORE BLOOD THERE WILL BE SHED IN MY NAME AND THE MORE SUBJECTS I WILL HAVE.

AND ALL THAT IS THANKS TO YOU, MIGUEL!

IF I HADN'T AGREED TO HELP YOU--

DON'T LOSE YOUR FAITH, MIGUEL. WITH OR WITHOUT YOU, THIS ALVAREZ PUPPET WOULD HAVE DONE HIS BIDDING.

NO! IT'S MY FAULT!

LET'S BURN IT ALL!

LET GO, IT'S MINE!

WANNA FIGHT?

NECOCYAOTL DIDN'T WASTE TIME...

THAT LOOKS LIKE A CIVIL WAR!

DOCTOR, PLEASE!

BRING A STRETCHER, QUICK!

TAKE OFF YOUR DIVINE ARMOR BEFORE ANYONE NOTICES!

EVERYONE IS TOO BUSY, BUT WE DON'T NEED TO TAKE ANY RISKS.

IT'S HANDY, ANYWAY!

MIGUEL? WHAT ARE YOU DOING HERE?

TIO? UHH... I...

PLAY THE PANIC CARD. HE WON'T ASK QUESTIONS.

IT'S JOAQUIM! HE'S HURT, HE...

OKAY, MIGUEL. CALM DOWN. I AM GOING TO CALL SOMEONE TO TAKE CARE OF HIM.

HOSPITAL SAN JOSE

THIS WAY! PLEASE!

ON SECOND THOUGHT, STAY HERE, OKAY? IT'S CRAZY IN THE CITY! THE PEOPLE OF THE SLUMS ARE DESCENDING ON THE CAPITAL AND HAVE STARTED TO LASH OUT AT ITS INHABITANTS AND LAW ENFORCEMENT. THEY HAVE BECOME CRAZY!

OKAY, TIO, THEN I WILL HEAD HOME.

REALLY?

BECAUSE OF THEM, WE HAD TO EVACUATE THE CENTER OF MEXICO CITY AND THE RIOTERS HAVE BLOCKED THE ACCESS TO IT AN—

AMBULAN

MIGUEL! BUT... I SAID TO STAY HERE.

YOU COULD HAVE WAITED UNTIL HE FINISHED HIS SENTENCE.

WE DON'T HAVE ANY MORE TIME TO LOSE. DON'T YOU GET IT?

GET WHAT?

IF THE POSSESSED PEOPLE OF THE SLUMS BLOCK THE ACCESS TO A QUARTER OF THE CITY, THAT'S WHERE NECOCYTHING MUST BE!

WHOOSH

IT MUST BE HERE...

LOOK! THERE HE IS! HE'S IN THE MIDDLE OF THAT EXCAVATION SITE.

"THESE ARE THE RUINS OF AN ANCIENT TEMPLE OF THE AZTEC CAPITAL, I THINK. IT WAS HERE UNTIL THE CONQUISTADORS... WELL, YOU KNOW THE HISTORY. THEY ARRIVED, THEY MASSACRED ALL THOSE THEY COULD, AND THEY TOOK POSSESSION OF THE AREA."

IT IS JUST ME OR HAS HE GROWN INCREDIBLY TALL ALL OF A SUDDEN?

HE'S GAINING POWER!

THE VIOLENCE AND THE BLOOD SHED BY HIS RIOTERS NOURISHES HIM. IF WE DON'T VANQUISH HIM QUICKLY, HE WILL SOON BE INVINCIBLE.

THIS IS ROUGH!

YOUR FRIENDS, YOUR NEIGHBORS, YOUR FAMILY! THEY ARE AT MY COMMAND NOW!

VLAM

FIGHT BACK, MIGUEL! I KNOW THAT YOU DON'T WANT TO HURT THESE PEOPLE, BUT IF YOU GIVE UP, NO ONE ELSE WILL BE ABLE TO OPPOSE NECOCYAOTL!

IF YOU DON'T DESTROY NECO, THESE PEOPLE WILL NEVER AGAIN BE FREE!

PAPI... EVERYONE... FORGIVE ME...

YAH!

GRAB HIM, SLAVES!

AND TAKE HIS WHIP. WITHOUT IT, HE CAN'T DO ANYTHING!

CAN'T FOOL ME TWICE, NECO!

PART 6 : NEO

Script by
PHILIPPE OGAKI

Art by
FRÉDÉRIC CHARVE

Color by
MAGALI PAILLAT

... AND THAT'S HOW THE JAPANESE ASTRONAUTS RETURNED FROM THEIR LONG VOYAGE ON MARS.

A GRAND RECEPTION WAS GIVEN IN THEIR HONOR AT THE *JAXA*, THE CENTER OF JAPANESE SPACE RESEARCH. HERE WE SAW ALL THE GENEROUS BENEFACTORS WITHOUT WHOM THE MISSION COULD NOT HAVE EXISTED.

CREEAK

NEO! TELL THIS UNFORTUNATE PERSON THAT *I'M* YOUR GIRLFRIEND!

NO, *I AM* YOUR GIRLFRIEND!

AND WHO ARE THE TWO OF YOU?

DROP DEAD, NEO!

OH, GIRLS... AT LEAST I GOT RID OF THEM.

SURE... IT'S FAKE, ALL THIS... I'LL GIVE YOU 20 EUROS FOR THE LOT OF IT.

WHAT?! TWENTY EUROS? BUT I RISKED MY LIFE TO FIND THESE THINGS AT THE BOTTOM OF THE SEA.

TAKE IT OR LEAVE IT!

YOU DIRTY CROOK!

?!

HIT ME, AND I ASSURE YOU THAT NO ONE IN TOWN WILL CONTINUE TO WANT TO BUY ANYTHING FROM YOU.

FINE.

ALL THESE FOOLS, I'LL MAKE THEM SEE!

BASSH

OWWW! COME ON! I CAN'T BELIEVE--

VRRRR

YEAH! COME ON, NEO!

ELIAS! GIVE HIM A RIGHT!

I WON'T LET YOU WIN, ELIAS!

YOU TALK TOO MUCH, NEO. IT DISTRACTS YOU FROM SEEING WHERE THE PUNCHES ARE COMING.

THAT MONEY WILL SOON BE MINE!

OUCH!

VICTORY FOR ELIAS BY K.O.!

YEAH!

KOF KOF!

SH-SHOOT!

TONIGHT ISN'T THE NIGHT YOU POCKET THE PRIZE MONEY, KID. COME SEE ME AGAIN WHEN YOU HAVE SOME HAIR ON YOUR CHIN.

THE POLICE! HURRY, GET OUT OF HERE!

BLAM

DON'T MOVE!

DON'T TIRE YOURSELF, WE ALREADY MISSED THEM! SOMEONE MUST HAVE WARNED THEM AGAIN...

FIGHT CLUBS ARE ILLEGAL, BUT EVER SINCE THE MOB TOOK OVER, IT'S BECOMING MORE AND MORE DIFFICULT TO FLUSH THEM OUT.

NEO? OH, MY GOD.

ARE YOU BLEEDING?! BUT WHO DID THIS TO YOU?!

IT'S NOTHING, MAMA. I JUST HAD A LITTLE FALL ON THE STAIRS AT SCHOOL.

THAT WOULD SURPRISE ME! *MRS. ZENOVIA*, YOUR HOMEROOM TEACHER, CALLED ME AT WORK TODAY. SHE TOLD ME THAT IT'S BEEN A WEEK SINCE SHE'S SEEN YOU AT SCHOOL. HOW DO YOU EXPLAIN THAT?

YOU BORE ME, MAMA!

MONEY? WHERE'S THAT FROM?

STOP ASKING QUESTIONS. WE NEED IT, THAT'S ALL. TAKE IT AND LET ME SHOWER.

NEO. ANSWER ME. I DON'T WANT DIRTY MONEY, DO YOU HEAR? REMEMBER YOUR FATHER...

YOUR FATHER NEVER SHOULD HAVE ASSOCIATED WITH THOSE FINANCIAL PEOPLE... BECAUSE OF THE ECONOMIC CRISIS, HE LOST EVERYTHING. ALL HIS DEBTS FORCED US TO GIVE UP THE BOAT CLUB AND OUR BEAUTIFUL HOUSE TO THAT CROOK SOPHOCLES.

WHY DO YOU HAVE TO KEEP HARPING ABOUT THIS?!

YOU LISTEN TO ME UNTIL I'M FINISHED. YOUR FATHER COULDN'T HANDLE THAT SITUATION AND IT KILLED HIM... AND FOR THE LAST YEAR, I'VE BEEN WORKING THREE JOBS SO THAT YOU AND YOUR BROTHERS AND SISTER CAN GO TO SCHOOL. I WANT YOU TO FINISH YOUR STUDIES TO LEARN A TRADE AND FIND A GOOD JOB, AND I WANT YOU TO BECOME AN HONEST MAN.

I WANT TO GET BACK TO HOW OUR LIVES WERE BEFORE, WHEN WE WERE RICH AND WHEN PAPA GAVE US EVERYTHING THAT WE WANTED! I'VE HAD ENOUGH OF THIS LIFE IN POVERTY.

HONESTY?! I HAVE NO DESIRE TO BE HONEST! I WANT MONEY, DO YOU HEAR ME? FOR YOU, FOR ME, AND FOR OUR FAMILY.

THIS MONEY, I DIDN'T STEAL IT IF YOU MUST KNOW.

NEO...

MAMA? NEO? YOU'RE MAKING TOO MUCH NOISE, WE CAN'T HEAR OUR TV SHOW!

AND WE'RE HUNGRY! WHEN DO WE EAT?

ME, I WANT A CAN OF SODA.

OH! LOOK, MONEY!

YIPEE!

WHOSE MONEY IS IT?

NO ONE'S, KOSMA.

SO, WE CAN TAKE IT?

OH, YES! WE WANT TO BUY SO MANY THINGS...

...THIS CELL PHONE!

THIS MONEY WILL NOT BE USED TO BUY THAT USELESS THING!

BUT EVERYONE AT SCHOOL HAS ONE...

CHILDREN! YOU CANNOT HAVE AS MANY THINGS AS BEFORE...

WE CAN NO LONGER LET YOU SPEND MONEY AS YOUR FATHER USED TO...

IT'S DIFFICULT ENOUGH JUST BUYING US ALL FOOD!

WE DON'T HAVE THE MONEY...

I DON'T LIKE BEING POOR...

ME NEITHER, IT'S DUMB!

WE MUST LOOK ON THE BRIGHT SIDE OF THINGS, *KYROS*.

WE ARE TOGETHER, AND WE HAVE A ROOF OVER OUR HEADS.

BAH... YOU'RE TALKING ABOUT JUST ANY HOUSE... ME, I WANT A BIG BEAUTIFUL ONE. LIKE OUR OLD VILLA.

YOU KNOW THAT'S NOT POSSIBLE, *KALLIOPE*...

ME, I WANT LUXURY! LIKE ON THE CRUISE LINER THAT JUST GOT INTO PORT!

IF ONLY WE COULD GO VISIT IT...

OH, YES, THAT WOULD BE THE BEST!

SETTLED! WE'LL GO TOMORROW.

THAT'S OUT OF THE QUESTION! I FORBID YOU TO DO THAT, DO YOU HEAR ME?

OH. LET THEM, MAMA...

NO! GO TO YOUR ROOM! ALL OF YOU! I NEED TO GET READY TO LEAVE FOR WORK.

AND YOU, NEO, I DO NOT WANT THAT MONEY!

WELL, GREAT, THEN YOU WON'T HAVE ANY MORE OF IT!

SLAM

NEO... I WOULD LIKE YOU TO GO BACK TO SCHOOL...

SHE DOESN'T UNDERSTAND ANYTHING.

STUDIES DON'T AMOUNT TO ANYTHING THESE DAYS.

SPLASH

SCHOOL IS FOR LOSERS!

IF YOU WANT SOMETHING, YOU HAVE TO TAKE IT WITH YOUR FISTS!

CRACK

NOT BAD! FINALLY AFTER TRAINING, I HAVE BECOME RATHER BULKY!

NEO, LISTEN TO ME, YOU ARE THE BEARER OF THE MARK, THE WORLD IS IN GREAT DANGER.

EVIL IS BACK, WE MUST HURRY.

SPLASH

WELL, I GUESS IF I'M HEARING VOICES, I MUST HAVE PUSHED MYSELF TOO HARD TONIGHT...

BUT I WILL SOON HAVE MY REVENGE ON ELIAS!

KYROS! KOSMA! KALLIOPE!

IT'S A TRUE HORROR STORY HITTING THE MARITIME COMPANIES OF THE MEDITERRANEAN SEA.

OVER THE LAST FEW DAYS, THIS IS THE NINTH ACCIDENT INVOLVING A SHIP.

THIS TIME, IT'S AN OIL TANKER.

ALL THESE SHIPS HAVE BEEN WRECKED AND DEFORMED IN AN INEXPLICABLE WAY. SEVERAL EMINENT ART CRITICS ARE ALREADY SUGGESTING THAT THIS MAY BE THE WORK OF A GREAT ANONYMOUS CONTEMPORARY ARTIST.

WHILE WE AWAIT EXPLANATIONS, RESCUE OPERATIONS HAVE BEGUN AS THE ENVIRONMENTAL REPERCUSSIONS ARE ALREADY PALPABLE.

NO ONE?! MY GOD!

NEO... NEO!

ЭMMH...Ɛ WHY ARE YOL SHOUTING SC LOUD?

YOU SPENT YOUR DAY SLEEPING INSTEAD OF GOING TO SCHOOL?

IT'S OKAY, MAMA, I WAS JUST--

WE'LL TALK ABOUT IT MORE LATER!

THERE'S SOMETHING MORE IMPORTANT: YOUR BROTHERS AND SISTER HAVE NOT COME BACK FROM SCHOOL. I'M SURE THEY WENT TO SEE THE CRUISE LINER! ONCE THEY HAVE AN IDEA IN THEIR HEADS...

GO BRING THEM BACK. AND HURRY, I KNOW THIS IS GOING TO END BADLY AGAIN!

IT'S FINE, MAMA, I'M GOING. DON'T WORRY TOO MUCH ABOUT THE KIDS. NOTHING WILL HAPPEN TO THEM.

EXCUSE ME, YOUNG MAN, WHERE DO YOU THINK YOU'RE GOING?

I NEED TO GET ON BOARD.

HEY, GUYS, EVERYTHING GOING ALRIGHT?

THAT'S IT!

WELL, IF YOU DON'T HAVE A TICKET, YOU CAN'T GO ABOARD. DO YOU HAVE A TICKET?

IT'S GOOD, BUT THIS HEAT!

HEY, NEO!

THE TRIPLETS...

DON'T GO AWAY SAD...

..JUST GO AWAY!

YOU'LL GET WHAT'S COMING TO YOU.

THEY'RE LIFTING THE ANCHORS? THE BOAT IS GOING TO LEAVE.

WHAT A HASSLE THE LITTLE PESTS PUTTING M[E] THROUGH. AGAIN!

≳MMM!≲ THIS CAKE IS SO GOOD.

YEAH, IT'S NOT BAD, BUT I PREFER THE CAVIAR TOASTS! NOW THAT'S A MEAL!

ME, I PREFER THE LOBSTER!

HEY! IS ANYONE THERE?! HELP US! WE'RE LOCKED IN, COME LET US OUT!

NEO! *NEO!* THERE'S WATER AT OUR FEET!

IT'S NO GOOD! NO ONE CAN HEAR US!

THE WATER'S RISING!

WE'RE GOING TO DROWN! HELP!

OH, REALLY?

I THOUGHT THAT I WOULDN'T BE ABLE TO MAKE CONTACT EVER AGAIN. YOU DON'T HAVE MIRRORS AT YOUR HOUSE? ANYWAY, LET'S MOVE ON TO THE SPECIFICS.

I AM *HERCULES*.

SPLASH

THAT'S POINTLESS... OKAY, LET ME EXPLAIN TWO OR THREE THINGS TO YOU... FIRST, I AM NOT REALLY HERE.

I'M IN THE SPIRIT WORLD. SO, PUNCHING THE WATER DOES NOTHING EXCEPT TO GET YOU EVEN MORE SOAKED.

SECOND, YOU ARE THE ONLY ONE WITH THE POWER TO SEE ME, SO IT'S USELESS TO SPEAK ALOUD.

AND THIRDLY, IF I'M HERE IT'S BECAUSE YOU ARE THE NEW HERO CHARGED TO FIGHT EVIL, AND WE DON'T HAVE MUCH TIME LEFT.

I DON'T KNOW WHO YOU ARE, GRAMPS, BUT HERE AND NOW, I'M JUST TRYING NOT TO DROWN WITH THE LITTLE ONES.

MY BAD! IF YOU DIE, YOU CAN'T FIGHT EVIL. SO, LET'S FIX THIS AS QUICKLY AS WE CAN. OKAY, DO WHAT I TELL YOU: OPEN THIS DOOR AND LEAVE!

ARE YOU STUPID?! YOU REALLY THINK THAT IF I WAS CAPABLE OF OPENING THIS DOOR, THAT I WOULD STAY HERE SPLASHING AROUND?

≥SIGH.≤

YOU'VE INHERITED MY STRENGTH. SO, YOU CA[N] TAKE THAT DOOR, PULL OFF ITS HINGES, AND LE[AVE] WITH YOUR FAMILY! D[O] YOU UNDERSTAND WHAT I'M TELLING YOU?

GO AHEAD, WITH A BIT OF GUSTO THIS TIME! I WOULD HAVE ALREADY SMASHED THIS WITH A FLICK OF MY WRIST!

OKAY, I GET IT!

SHUT IT, LION-O!

CRACK

PLOOSH

LET'S GO, KIDS! WE'RE GETTING OUT OF HERE!

I TOLD YOU THAT NEO WASN'T ALL THERE! HE'S TALKING TO HIMSELF!

SHH, KALLIOPE, HE'S GOING TO HEAR YOU!

TOTALLY FREAKY, BRO!

WE'RE IN THE KITCHENS!

THE RECEPTION HALL IS THROUGH HERE, WE CAN EXIT THIS WAY!

HELP!

BRRM

THE ENTIRE FRONT OF THE BOAT IS UNDERWATER. WE CAN'T GET OUT THAT WAY.

BUT WE WERE JUST IN THE HOLD, AND EVERYTHING THERE IS UNDERWATER!

DO YOU THINK WE'RE GOING TO DIE, NEO?

NO, I DON'T WANT TO DIE.

OKAY, KID,

WHAT ARE YOU WAITING FOR?

ARE YOU GOING TO BOTHER ME AGAIN?! THERE ISN'T AN EXIT, AND I'M TRYING TO THINK.

BUT IT'S NOT POSSIBLE! MY DESCENDANT CAN'T BE THIS STUPID! I TOLD YOU THAT YOU HAVE MY STRENGTH! HERCULES, DOESN'T THAT NAME MEAN ANYTHING TO YOU?

WELL... NO!

WELL... I'LL EXPLAIN IT TO YOU, IF THERE'S NO WAY TO GET OUT, THEN YOU MAKE ONE! YOU TAKE YOUR LITTLE FISTS AND YOU MAKE A HOLE IN THIS WALL!

BONK

NO, THE DOOR IS ONE THING, BUT HERE, IT'S DIFFERENT. IT'S TOO SOLID!

ALL THAT'S IN YOUR HEAD, THERE IS NO DIFFERENCE. TRUST ME! LET'S GO, STRIKE IT WITH THE CONVICTION THAT YOU CAN PIERCE THE WALL.

LET'S GO! YOU CAN DO IT, KID! IT'S JUST LIKE THE DOOR!

CRACK

THAT'S NOT BAD, KID!

I'M NOT A KID, AND MY NAME IS NEO!

!!!

WHAT IS THIS INSANITY...?

CRASH

THAT IS A VERY, VERY BIG PROBLEM!

THAT'S *ARES*, ONE OF THE INCARNATIONS OF EVIL. WE MUST BE VERY--

UH... VERY PRUDENT!

CRIII

WHO?

WHO DARES TO DISTRACT ME IN THE MIDDLE OF MY CREATIVE INSPIRATION?!

TCHACK

HEY! WAKE UP, WE'RE HOME!

OH, THANK GOD! YOU ARE ALL SAFE AND SOUND!

I WAS SO NERVOUS, I SAW THE SINKING OF THE LINER ON THE TV!

IF SOMETHING HAD HAPPENED TO YOU, I--

YOU ARE COMPLETELY THOUGHTLESS! I FORBADE YOU FROM GOING ON THAT BOAT!

BUT, MAMA--

NOT A WORD. GO TO YOUR ROOMS. WE'LL TALK ABOUT IT TOMORROW, WHEN YOU HAVE RESTED.

BUT! WELL, OKAY... GOODNIGHT, MAMA.

NEO... THANK YOU FOR BRINGING THEM HOME.

IT WAS NOTHING, MAMA... IN FACT, MAY I BORROW YOUR MIRROR?

YOU ARE SO RECKLESS! YOU MUST FOLLOW MY INSTRUCTIONS IF YOU WANT TO DESTROY EVIL.

HEY, CALM DOWN, OLD MAN! WHO SAID I WANTED TO FIGHT THIS EVIL?

EXCUSE ME? YOU ARE A HERO NOW! WHAT IS MORE IMPORTANT THAN SAVING HUMANITY?!

BUT YOU THREW A BENCH AT HIS FACE!

YEAH! THAT GUY IN RED WAS REALLY GETTING ON MY NERVES! IF I SEE HIM AGAIN, I WILL BASH HIS HEAD IN, BUT I'M NOT GOING TO TIRE MYSELF OUT CHASING AFTER HIM ANY LONGER. I'VE GOT MORE IMPORTANT THINGS TO DO!

YOU DON'T STOP!

THE GUY LIKES TO BREAK BOATS. SO LONG AS I'M NOT ON THEM, I'M NOT CONCERNED.

AND EVEN BETTER, IF HE COULD SINK THE BOATS THAT BELONG TO THAT SCUMBAG SOPHOCLES, THAT HELPS ME OUT.

SO YOU HAVE NO INTENTION OF HELPING ME FIGHT AND DESTROY ARES?

WHY WOULD I? WHAT WOULD I GET OUT OF IT?

BUT... BUT YOU ARE THE BEARER OF THE MARK!

YOU'RE THE NEW HERO!

FINE! THAT'S IT, NEO! NOW, GIVE ME A LITTLE VITAL ENERGY SO THAT I CAN MATERIALIZE IN THE HUMAN WORLD!

SHUT IT, I'M SLEEPING!

HOW DARE Y--

129

CRASH

THE BOSS IS GOING TO END UP BREAKING THE ENTIRE ISLAND INTO PIECES IF THIS CONTINUES.

YEAH, BUT IT WAS ALREADY IN RUINS.

DOES ANYONE KNOW WHY HE'S SO UPSET?

CRAC

I'D SAY, IT'S BETTER FOR HIM TO LET OFF STEAM ON THE ROCKS INSTEAD OF ON US!

EH, HE'S ALWAYS UPSET...

CRUSH

I NEEDED TO GET BACK IN THE RHYTHM.

WELL, WELL... THAT'S BETTER!

I CAN'T EVEN HANDLE A LITTLE TWERP WHO CAME TO RUIN MY DAY WHILE I WAS RELAXING BY DISMANTLING MY LITTLE BOAT.

I AM SO MISUNDER-STOOD!

WHAT I'M MAKING, HOWEVER, IS ART!

THE ART... OF WAR!

IT'S TIME TO PREPARE MY GREATEST WORK. DO YOU HAVE ANY NEWS OF THE ARTIFACT?

YES, BOSS. WE'VE FOUND IT. IT IS UNDER THE OLYMPIC RUINS. THEY'VE BEEN ABANDONED.

WE CAN GO THERE WITHOUT ANYONE DISTURBING US.

THE PROBLEM IS THAT THE THING WEIGHS TONS. ALSO, IT'S HIDDEN DEEP BENEATH THE EARTH. TO UNEARTH IT AND GET IT OUT WILL NOT BE EASY!

THESE DETAILS BORE ME. SINCE YOU ARE NOTHING BUT A GROUP OF INCOMPETENTS, I'M GOING TO HELP YOU.

THERE'S ALSO THE PROBLEM OF THE ACTIVATOR...

HMMM... I THINK THAT A SOLUTION PRESENTED ITSELF TO ME TODAY...

130

I PULVERIZED THIS BLOCK OF STONE AND I DON'T HAVE EVEN A SCRATCH ON ME!

I'VE BECOME SUPER STRONG!

YEAH! SUPER STRONG!

SPLASH

WHAT THE--?! WHY DID I WEAKEN ALL OF A SUDDEN?!

WHEN YOU'RE DONE PLAYING WITH STONES, MAYBE WE COULD GET TO WORK?!

WE MUST FIGHT EVIL!

BUT, YOU'RE STILL THERE? HOW CAN I SAY THIS NICELY? I DON'T WORK FOR YOU!

BUT YOU RECEIVED YOUR STRENGTH FOR THIS PURPOSE!

NOPE, I DON'T THINK SO!

ON THE OTHER HAND, I THINK THAT I'VE FOUND A MUCH MORE PROFITABLE WAY TO USE THIS NEW POWER.

I DON'T LIKE THE SOUND OF THAT...

131

AND THAT'S THE TENTH VICTORY IN A ROW FOR NEO TONIGHT!

ARE THERE ANY OTHER VOLUNTEERS TO CONFRONT HIM?

COME ON, NO ONE? ONE MORE MATCH!

THERE'S MONEY TO BE MADE!

I'M READY TO FIGHT YOU, NEO.

LET'S SEE IF YOU ARE A FAILURE LIKE YOUR FATHER.

SOPHOCLES! I AM GOING TO MAKE YOU SWALLOW YOUR TEETH AS WELL AS YOUR WORDS!

LET'S MAKE THIS MORE INTERESTING. DOUBLE OR NOTHING!

I WILL AVENGE MY FAMILY!

THAT'S GOOD, YOU'RE NOT A WEAKLING, NEO. BUT I'M GOING TO SHOW YOU WHAT TRUE STRENGTH IS!

THAT'S NOT BAD, MY BOY! YOU HAVE A GOOD RIGHT BUT IT'S NOT QUITE ENOUGH TO BEAT ME!

BAM

VICTORY TO MR. SOPHOCLES!

IT'S NOT POSSIBLE!

DESPITE ALL THE POWER THAT I RECEIVED, I WAS CRUMBLED LIKE A PITA!

YOU FOUGHT WELL JUST NOW, NEO!

SOPHOCLES! WHAT DO YOU WANT FROM ME?!

I LIKE YOUR COMBATIVENESS! I HAVE A PROPOSITION TO MAKE TO YOU.

I NEED STRONG MEN LIKE YOU, NEO.

WORK FOR ME AND YOU WILL BE RICHER THAN YOU CAN IMAGINE.

WE ARE OF THE SAME FABRIC, NEO. WE ARE THE STRONG ONES!

JOIN ME AND WE WILL REIGN OVER THE WORLD!

NEO! GET INSIDE RIGHT NOW!

AND YOU, MISTER SOPHOCLES, I URGE YOU TO LEAVE US IN PEACE!

WE WANT NOTHING TO DO WITH A CROOK LIKE YOU!

I HATE HIM! WHY COULDN'T I BEAT HIM?

YOU KNOW YOU'RE THE WORST HERO IN HISTORY? WE DON'T CARE ABOUT YOUR SOPHOCLES. YOU MUST STOP EVIL, IT'S BECOMING URGENT!

YOU JUST WON'T LET IT GO, OLD MAN?!

NO, NOT UNTIL YOU'VE VANQUISHED EVIL. BUT YOU STILL NEED TO GET SOME MORE POWER AND FOR THAT, WE NEED THE LEGENDARY WEAPON.

WHOA, WHOA, WAIT!... DID YOU SAY, MORE POWER?

UH, YEAH, IT'S EVIDENT THAT YOU DON'T AT ALL MEASURE UP IN SIZE TO ARES, SO...

OKAY, DEAL! WHAT DO I DO?!

DO WE AGREE: YOU'RE READY TO FULFILL YOUR ROLE AS HERO?

OH, YEAH, GRAMPS! LET'S HEAR IT, TELL ME WHERE TO FIND THIS WEAPON.

BEFORE ALL ELSE, REACH YOUR HAND TO ME AND GIVE ME A LITTLE OF YOUR VITAL ENERGY.

WHAT? ARE YOU SAYING THAT YOU'RE GOING TO SPOIL MY LIFE FOREVER NOW?!

IF YOU'D TOLD ME THAT, I NEVER WOULD HAVE GIVEN YOU ANYTHING!

THAT'S EXACTLY WHY I DIDN'T TELL YOU THAT! WELL, CAN WE GO NOW?

IN THIS FORM, I CAN WATCH OVER ALL THAT YOU DO.

YOU KNOW THAT YOU LOOK REALLY RIDICULOUS LIKE THAT?

YEAH, THANKS, I'VE NOTICED!

I REALLY MISS MY EXCELLENT MUSCLES!

AFTER OUR VICTORY OVER EVIL, I ENTERED HERE AND PUT THE WEAPON THAT CHANNELS MY POWER IN THE GREATEST OF TEMPLES!

I WAS SURE THAT SUCH AN EDIFICE WOULD PROTECT IT FOR ETERNITY...

...

BUT...

BUT... IT'S MISSING ITS ROOF?!

GREAT, AND NOW, WHERE IS THIS WEAPON?

IT'S NOT POSSIBLE! EVERYTHING'S IN RUINS! WHAT HAVE YOU DONE IN MY ABSENCE TO DESTROY ONE OF THE SEVEN WONDERS OF THE WORLD?!

ARE YOU DONE COMPLAINING NOW? WHAT'S DONE IS DONE. LET'S GO, I MUST BECOME A HERO.

YOU'RE RIGHT! FOLLOW ME.

HERE IT IS, BOSS!

BUT *POSEIDON* HAD IT BURIED HUNDREDS OF FEET UNDER GROUND.

WE CAN'T DO ANYTHING WITH OUR SHORT ARMS!

I'M GOING TO HAVE TO DO EVERYTHING MYSELF, LIKE ALWAYS!

YOU ARE TRULY USELESS TO ME!

CRACK

BOOM

THERE IT IS! TAKE IT AND BRING IT TO THE ISLAND!

BUT WE'LL BURN OUR-SELVES?!

POOR IMBECILES, YOU'RE NOTHING BUT A HEAP OF BONES... YOU CAN'T BURN YOURSELVES! NOW, GO!

THIS ISN'T A LEGIT JOB! WE SHOULD HAVE THE RIGHT TO WORKERS' COMPENSATION!

YEAH, AND HE ALWAYS TALKS TO US IN SUCH AN AGGRESSIVE WAY.

AS SOON AS WE'RE BACK, I PROPOSE THAT WE GO ON STRIKE!

THEY SAY ON THE NEWS THAT THERE WAS A VOLCANIC ERUPTION AT THE OLYMPIC SITE!

MY GOD!

MY FAMILY LIVES IN THAT AREA!

THAT'S THE WORK OF ARES, I HAVE NO DOUBT! COME ON, LET'S GO, KID!

IT'S TIME TO SEE IF YOU HAVE TRULY MASTERED YOUR NEW STRENGTH!

THAT'S ALMOST 10 MILES FROM HERE! HOW CAN I GET THERE?

IT'S NOT ONLY IN YOUR ARMS THAT YOU POSSES THIS STRENGTH! USE YOUR LEGS! IN A COUPLE OF LEAPS, YOU WILL BE THERE.

WE MUST BLOCK THE PATH!

IF WE DON'T INTERVENE QUICKL' THE LAVA MIGHT CO\ THE WHOLE CITY.

MAMA!

CRUSH

FSSHH

WELL PLAYED, KID!

I USED THE SAME METHOD TO CLEAN THE STABLES! THE GOOD OLD WAY, THAT'S ALL THERE TRULY IS!

PERFECT! I OULD HAVE BEEN ISAPPOINTED IF YOU HADN'T SHOWN UP!

I AM GOING TO CRUSH YOU THIS TIME.

BLAM

WELL... YOU HAVE GOTTEN STRONGER FROM WHAT I CAN TELL.

LET ME LIBERATE U FROM YOUR CHAINS ND YOU WILL BECOME EN MORE POWERFUL!

CRASH

CRACK

PAY ATTENTION, KID! YOUR BATTLE PUTS PEOPLE IN DANGER!

GIVE ME A BREAK, OLD MAN!

I FINALLY HAVE THE CHANCE TO SETTLE MY AFFAIRS, NOTHING WILL GET IN MY WAY!

BAM

NO!

BOOM

142

143

EVERYTHING IS READY, BOSS!

THE GONG IS IN PLACE.

PERFECT! AND MY GUEST IS ARRIVING. IT'S GOING TO BE MAGNIFICENT!

I FEEL INSPIRATION COMING! I SEE A VIBRANT WORK OF FEAR AND DESPAIR!

I WILL NEVER FORGIVE YOU FOR WHAT YOU DID TO MY MOTHER!

NO, NEO! DON'T FALL INTO HIS TRAP!

BUT IT'S NOT MY FAULT, BOY

ALL I DID WAS DEFLECT THE CAR THAT YOU THREW AT MY HEAD!

HAVE YOU THOUGHT ABOUT MY OFFER?

GO NG

I'M GOING TO MAKE A PASTA DISH OUT OF YOUR CALAMARI!

CRAC

WHO ARE YOU BETTING ON?

I PUT FIVE BONES ON THE OCTOPUS.

DO YOU THINK WE CAN BET AGAINST THE BOSS?

SLASH

AND HERE I THOUGHT YOU WOULD JOIN ME...

BUT YOU DON'T KNOW HOW TO SEIZE OPPORTUNITIES, IN THE END YOU'RE NOTHING BUT A WEAKLING...

LIKE YOUR FATHER, NEO!

WHAT?...

YOU... YOU ARE SOPHOCLES?!

SPLASH

THERE, THAT'S HOW I SEIZE OPPORTUNITIES!

CONGRATULATIONS, KID! YOU'RE A HERO AFTER ALL!

BUT YOU SHOULD FISH HIM OUT AND TAKE CARE OF THE PRISONERS AND THINK OF GETTING RID OF THAT GONG.

THAT'S FINE, BUT COULD YOU LET ME CATCH MY BREATH FOR FIVE MINUTES. I ALMOST JUST DIED IF YOU RECALL!

HEY! I TOLD YOU IT WAS A TRAP!

YOU'RE ALWAYS RIGHT, HUH?

WATCH OUT FOR PAPERCUT

Welcome to the surprising sophomore edition of THE MYTHICS, "Teenage Gods," by Patrick Sobral, Patricia Lyfoung, Philippe Ogaki, Alice Picard, Jérôme Alquié, and Frédéric Charve, from Papercutz—those mere mortals dedicated to publishing great graphic novels for all ages. I'm Jim Salicrup, the Editor-in-Chief and God of Typos, here to tell you about other Papercutz graphic novels you might enjoy if you loved THE MYTHICS…

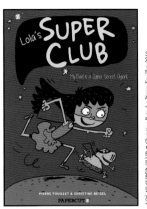

Unlike Yuko, Amir, Abigail (you remember them from THE MYTHICS #1, right?), Parvati, Miguel, and Neo, most of us can only dream about being granted great powers and having incredible adventures. But some of our dreams may be more vivid and exciting than others. For example, there's Lola, the star of the new Papercutz graphic novel series LOLA'S SUPER CLUB, and she imagines truly amazing adventures featuring her toys and cat, Hot Dog. In LOLA'S SUPER CLUB #1 "My Dad is a Super Secret Agent," Lola imagines her dad is James Blond, the famous super-spy, and that Max Imus and his double-O agents (Zero + Zero) are after him. It's up to Super-Lola, in her tutu, along with Super-James, in his undies, Hot Dog, and a whole bunch of super-friends to save her dad. In the very same graphic novel, Super-Lola and her Super Club must also save her mom, who is somehow trapped in time by Max Imus. Her time-travels are especially fun for Papercutz fans, as she visits 50 BC, the time the ASTERIX graphic novel series is set in, and she even meets a somewhat sillier version of Quetzalcoatl back in 1492. He's not exactly like the Quetzalcoatl that Miguel met in this graphic novel, but you know how those feathered serpent gods can be, right?

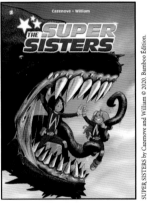

If you enjoy Lola's imaginary adventures that she dreams up, you may also enjoy THE SISTERS by Cazenove and William, the Papercutz graphic novel series about sisters Wendy and Maureen, who lead fairly ordinary lives driving each other crazy, but then they also imagine themselves as the Super Sisters, and have awesome real-life inspired adventures. These mini-adventures are so popular within their already super popular series, that an entire graphic novel has been created by Cazenove and William devoted exclusively to their super-hero fantasies, Naturally it's called THE SUPER SISTERS, and it's a lot of fun, even if at times they seem to be fighting more with each other than their actual villains.

There's another new Papercutz graphic novel series that's just about the opposite of LOLA'S SUPER CLUB and THE SUPER SISTERS, it's about a girl named Tara Smith who for years was living a life that she believed was real, but it was totally false. She believed her parents were her parents, but they weren't. And she thought she was just a regular human girl. She's not. To find out the shocking reality of Tara's life, check out SCHOOL FOR EXTRATER-RESTRIAL GIRLS #1 "Girl on Fire," by Jeremy Whitley and Jamie Noguchi, available at booksellers everywhere. There's also a special preview on page 153.

But back to THE MYTHICS. Now that you've met the six chosen ones, the big question is what's next? Or as Hercules said: WHAT?! The answer is that Evil isn't defeated yet, so our heroes still have a lot of work to do. So, we're finally going to start seeing our young heroes meet each other in THE MYTHICS #3 "Apocalypse Ahead,"* coming soon. You don't want to miss it!

Thanks,

LOLA'S SUPER CLUB © Christine Beigel + Pierre Fouillet, 2010. © Bang. Ediciones, segunda edición 2017–2020.

SUPER SISTERS by Cazenove and William © 2020. Bamboo Édition.

SCHOOL FOR EXTRATERRESTRIAL GIRLS © Jeremy Whitley and Jamie Noguchi.

STAY IN TOUCH!

EMAIL: salicrup@papercutz.com
WEB: www.papercutz.com
TWITTER: @papercutzgn
FACEBOOK: PAPERCUTZGRAPHICNOVELS
REGULAR MAIL: Papercutz, 160 Broadway, Suite 700, East Wing, New York, NY 10038

*If that title sounds a bit familiar it's because I mistakenly said in THE MYTHICS #1 that it was the title for this volume. Oopsie.

Special preview of SCHOOL FOR EXTRATERRESTRIAL GIRLS #1 "Girl on Fire"...

MY FATHER ONCE SAID TO ME, "*TARA, ESTABLISHING A ROUTINE IS THE MOST IMPORTANT THING YOU CAN DO.*"

"*ESTABLISHING A ROUTINE AND STICKING TO IT WILL MAKE EVERY OTHER ASPECT OF YOUR LIFE EASIER.*"

"*AND ONCE EVERYTHING IS MADE SIMPLER, YOU'LL BE READY TO ACCOMPLISH GREAT THINGS.*"

BEEP BEEP BEEP BEEP

06:00 AM

IT'S A PRETTY SIMPLE PIECE OF ADVICE, ALL THINGS CONSIDERED.

CLICK

MOST TEENAGERS JUST AREN'T CLEVER OR DISCIPLINED ENOUGH TO STICK TO IT.

BUT MY PARENTS HAVE FAITH IN ME. THEY HAVE WORKED VERY HARD TO MAKE A WORLD POSSIBLE WHERE I CAN HAVE A ROUTINE THAT LEADS TO SUCCESS.

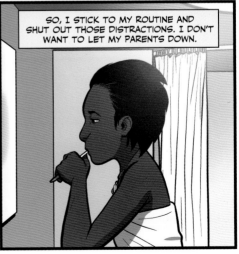

SO, I STICK TO MY ROUTINE AND SHUT OUT THOSE DISTRACTIONS. I DON'T WANT TO LET MY PARENTS DOWN.

FOR MY PARENTS, ROUTINE ISN'T JUST SOMETHING THEY PUSH ON ME, IT'S SOMETHING THEY LIVE BY.

BY THE TIME I WAKE UP FOR SCHOOL, MY PARENTS HAVE ALREADY LEFT FOR THEIR JOBS, SO IT'S IMPORTANT THAT THEY CAN TRUST ME TO STICK TO MY ROUTINE.

FOR EXAMPLE, BREAKFAST IS THE MOST IMPORTANT MEAL OF THE DAY. IF I SKIP IT, I'LL BE LESS ATTENTIVE IN SCHOOL.

6:27

MY PARENTS LEAVE SPECIFIC FOODS FOR ME, BECAUSE I HAVE A NUMBER OF ALLERGIES AND EATING THE WRONG THING COULD CAUSE PROBLEMS.

THAT'S ALSO WHY I TAKE SO MANY MEDICATIONS. IF I MISSED ONE, IT COULD HAVE TERRIBLE EFFECTS ON MY HEALTH.

LIKE I SAID, I HAVE A LOT OF ALLERGIES.

I EVEN HAVE THIS BRACELET. I'M NOT REALLY SURE HOW IT WORKS, BUT MY PARENTS SAY IT'S VITAL TO MY HEALTH TO KEEP IT ON.

SO, I DO. IT'S IMPORTANT TO DO AS YOU'RE TOLD.

BUT FIRST, I JUST HAVE TO MAKE IT THROUGH HIGH SCHOOL.

THAT'S NOT AS EASY AS IT SOUNDS, BUT I'VE ADAPTED.

IF YOU ESTABLISH A SOUND ENOUGH ROUTINE AND STICK TO IT, YOU CAN MAKE IT THROUGH ANYTHING.

IT CAN GET LONELY, BUT LIKE MY PARENTS SAY, THOSE OTHER KIDS ARE DISTRACTIONS.

I KEEP MY HEAD DOWN. I KEEP TO THE ROUTINE. I LEARN SCIENCE AND MATH WHILE THEY GOOF OFF.

I'M WORKING ON BECOMING EXTRAORDINARY. THEY'RE JUST...

LET'S PLAY POKE THE WEIRD GIRL! *POKE!*

...ORDINARY TEENAGERS, I GUESS.

IN THE EVENINGS, I SEE MY PARENTS FOR THE FIRST TIME AT DINNER.

EVERY DINNER IS ESSENTIALLY THE SAME.

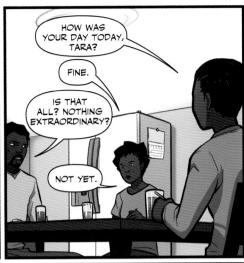

HOW WAS YOUR DAY TODAY, TARA?

FINE.

IS THAT ALL? NOTHING EXTRAORDINARY?

NOT YET.

THEN, ONCE DINNER IS FINISHED, I START WORKING ON MY HOMEWORK.

MY FATHER LOOKS OVER MY GRADED WORK TO SEE WHERE I'VE FAILED.

MY MOTHER CHECKS THE WORK AS I DO IT TO MAKE SURE IT'S CORRECT.

YOU'VE MISSPELLED THESE FIVE WORDS. YOU'LL NEED TO PRACTICE WRITING THEM ONE HUNDRED TIMES EACH.

AND YOU'LL NEED TO CORRECT YOUR MATH HERE.

YES, SIR.

YES, MA'AM.

THEN, AFTER ALL OF MY SCHOOLWORK IS DONE, I TAKE OUT THE TRASH.

IT MAY SEEM STRANGE TO YOU, BUT THIS IS MY FAVORITE PART OF THE DAY FOR ONE REASON.

Don't miss the rest of SCHOOL FOR EXTRATERRESTRIAL GIRLS available now at booksellers and libraries everywhere.